A *Dire Wolves* MISSION

Savage Salvation

A *Dire Wolves* MISSION

ELLIS LEIGH

Kinship Press

Savage Salvation: A Dire Wolves Mission
Copyright © 2019 by Ellis Leigh
All rights reserved.

First Edition

ISBN
978-1-944336-77-6

Kinship Press
P.O. Box 221
Prospect Heights, IL 60070

Pride makes us long for a solution to things — a solution, a purpose, a final cause; but the better telescopes become, the more stars appear.

— JULIAN BARNES

One

Rage. The emotion ate away at an existence until there was little to nothing left, until all the peace and joy in the world had been devoured. Fueled by hate and heat, by the disappointment of one's own life and the knowledge that the end was bearing down, there was nothing that could calm it, nothing that could make the inferno burning within subside. There were only distractions.

Scaring humans who should know better than to do what they were doing was one of Luc's favorite distractions.

"Holy shit, that's a huge wolf."

Luc didn't move, didn't even twitch an ear. Yes, he was a huge wolf. A Dire Wolf, to be exact. An ancient breed long thought to be extinct that had hunted and killed much larger animals than themselves across tundra and glacier and places far less hospitable than around the Arctic Circle in Alaska. He had no reason to prove that fact. Yet.

"What's he doing out there?"

"Sitting. The damn thing ain't moving."

No need to move, though he would be soon enough. The men were staying in a cabin where they didn't belong, hunting animals who weren't to be hunted. Their excitement had woken Luc from a dead sleep, and their other emotions had intrigued him enough to put off his own hunting for the morning to come on this trek. Excitement, arrogance, and a covetous sort of entitlement—he sensed a lot more than just those, but that's what had enticed him. That's what had told him these were not your average hunters. That's what had distracted him from the rage constantly brewing under his skin.

"Send out the dogs."

"Are you crazy? He'll eat them for a snack, then come for us."

Luc may not have been a fan of dogs, the human pets too loud and brash for his preference, but he wouldn't eat them. He wouldn't even kill them unless they somehow managed to become a threat. Considering he was likely six or seven times their size if they were sled dogs, he doubted they'd be anything more than a nuisance.

The fear inside the cabin grew, the sensation scratching along Luc's spine. Good. Let those men be scared. Let them be terrified by the black wraith who lived in the spruce forests near the Arctic Circle. Let them struggle with their own mortality in relation to the beast he'd become—so long as they stayed away from the quarry they sought, his job could be called complete. For the moment.

A hundred thoughts and emotions coursed over his skin, slipped inside his brain and took up space. Implanted themselves in his own emotional core and left him with a confusing sort of mishmash that buried his own feelings somewhere too deep to find. Luc hated to be this close to human civilization, not that there were many places left to escape it. He wanted to be farther north, deeper into the uninhabitable parts of Alaska. Living on the land humans passed over. Alas, he'd been brought down to the Brooks Range area by the sensation of something not quite right. Of a shadow of evil covering the land. He'd been following the local pack there for many, many moons and had been stuck feeling all the human emotions of the tourists, the truckers, the native tribes. He had been buried in sensations that were not his own for far too long, which did nothing to stop the rage from building.

These poachers had been his last straw.

"We can't hunt with that thing lurking."

"We'll wait him out. Johnson wants those bear cubs dead—no wolf is going to get in my way. I don't care how big the fucker is."

If Luc had been in his human form, he would have been grinning. Wait him out? These men had no idea who or what they were dealing with.

They would learn.

Two days. The humans' waiting game lasted a total of two days before their anxious, jumpy energy finally exploded into some sort of action.

"I'm going out there."

"Are you stupid? That thing has to be twice your size."

"So? I've got a gun. I just need to get close enough for it to matter."

Luc let an ear twitch, allowed himself that slight movement. It wasn't for the humans, though. His packmates were close. Phego and Michaela had tracked him down, inching closer as the hours had passed. He could practically taste their worry, feel their sense of duty and family driving them closer. He didn't want them near these humans, but he didn't have a way to stop them without ruining his game. He had to trust his Dire brother to keep the shewolf safe while Luc dealt with the humans. Then he would follow them back to camp. Back to the endless percussion of others' emotions and the puzzle of what was wrong in those mountains that he couldn't seem to solve.

The door to the cabin suddenly opened, all thoughts of anything other than the hunter on the porch disappearing. Luc dug his claws into the mossy ground, ready to lunge. Not much longer now. The human would move closer, aiming his rifle at the threat of Luc's huge, black wolf. That would be Luc's opportunity—his moment to terrify the men into leaving the Range. That was all he was waiting for.

"Holy shit," the man with the gun said, looking past Luc. Likely seeing the eyes or shadows of the two wolves still tucked away in the thicker, older trees. "There are more of them."

The man's fear ratcheted up to near panic, his entire essence turning into a scrabbling sense of self-preservation that burned its way across Luc's bones. Not wanting to miss the party, Luc slowly rose to his paws, giving his huge body the time it deserved to unfold, giving the man a show. They thought he was big lying down—they had no idea much they'd missed.

"Dear god." The man stumbled backward, gun in his hand likely forgotten. Luc took a single step, his mouth watering as the man's fight-or-flight response triggered Luc's hunting instincts. He could feel Phego growing closer, knew he'd be forced to rein in his beast soon enough. But until then...

The man moved his arm. It was a single moment, less than a second, and something that may have been a twitch. May have been the man prepping to raise his weapon. Whatever it was about the arm movement that flipped Luc's switch from torment to target, his reaction came immediately. He was running before the man could even move, growling and snarling as he headed directly toward the human. The man fell back, the scent of urine overpowering everything else as his body released on itself. Luc didn't stop, though. He pounced on the fallen human, showing his teeth. Growling low and deep and letting the man know exactly the sort of creature he'd decided to tangle with.

A growl from the woods behind him pulled Luc up short, though. That wasn't Phego—that was Michaela, his Dire brother's mate. A shewolf he respected and considered pack. He lifted his head, turning in her direction. The gray wolf—much smaller than her mate and damn near tiny in comparison to to Luc—slunk out of the woods, staring him down. She looked serious, which meant Luc's game with the humans was over.

Or at least it would be once he made his point.

Without warning, Luc jumped on the man, lowering his massive head, snarling viciously as he let his mouth water. Let the drool pass through his teeth and hang there. Let it fall into the man's face. The human recoiled, shaking and breathing way too hard. His friend never stepped foot outside, but Luc could sense his panic. Could practically taste the determination inside him. That man was leaving, and the one on the ground needed to go with him.

Another growl from Michaela and Luc backed off. Retreating slowly from the would-be poachers. Not turning his back on the one with the gun until he reached the denser tree line. Slipping into the shadows of the woods with his pack.

As soon as Luc disappeared into the darkness, the man on the ground jumped to his feet and ran toward the cabin, his pants soaking wet and his face red. He stumbled twice, nearly falling up the steps leading to the porch, before throwing the door open and racing inside.

"That's it." The door slammed behind him, the sound

of his footsteps hard and fast as he moved through the little structure.

"Holy shit, what happened out there?"

"What happened? I was almost eaten, or did you not see that wolf pin me down?"

"Fuck, we need to get out of here."

"You don't have to tell me twice. Load up—we're taking the snow machines back to town. Johnson can deal with those bears on his own."

Satisfied for the moment, Luc practically skipped toward his packmates, bumping into Michaela softly along the way. The shewolf snorted her irritation but followed her Alpha through the woods. Back to the mountains where Luc's world had begun to unravel, his skills tested and coming up lacking.

To where he was certain there were female wolves being held against their will, but nothing he did to locate them worked.

The sense of failure rode him hard, overcoming all the other emotional input from the area and demanding Luc experience it. Demand he pay his penance for not working fast enough, smart enough, hard enough. The hunters no longer mattered, the bear cubs he'd saved forgotten. There was nothing for him to hold on to except for the sensation that he would never fix what he needed to. That he was only making things worse by throwing such negative energy into the world. That he should give up and lumber off into the more desolate spaces to be alone. To surrender to the exhaustion that haunted him. To give up.

Luc was not a quitter, though. He would find those women, and then…

Death had been a long time coming for him.

Luc could not afford any more distractions—he had a job to do.

One he'd been failing at for over a year.

One that only made the rage within him burn that much hotter.

One that, once solved, might bring him peace for the first time in his very long life. Even if that peace was final.

— —

Alaska. The frozen north. The land of the endless night and the midnight sun. The ruggedness of the place had always called to Luc, the scent of the holy wild filling him in a way few things could. Reminding him of the land where he'd been born so many hundreds of years before. His appetite for life increased when he crossed over the invisible Arctic Circle and he stood deep in the wilderness of Alaska. His connection to the earth grew stronger with every step, firmly rooting in his soul and tugging his human side closer to the great wolf who'd guided him since birth. The spirit who shared his consciousness. The one who suffered under the burdens the fates had bestowed on him.

But Alaska also offered him space and perspective, relief from the hecticness that came with a more crowded area. The place gave him the power to see the world for what it was, to sense the seasonal rhythms of the wild around him, and to expand his natural empathic sensibilities to a new level. The Alaskan bush made Luc feel more powerful than he ever had before, even as he hunted for women who might not exist, continually failing in his quest.

Years. He'd spent what felt like years in these forests. Well, not these particularly—he'd only come to the Brooks Range the year before, having been farther north for a time before that. He'd stumbled on to a pack here, though. One that had left him with an impression of sickness. Of vileness. Of something dead and rotting in their hearts. They'd claimed to have two women in their midst, a fact Luc had confirmed when he'd sensed the feminine energy near them. He'd been hunting for them—or any hint of that female energy within the pack—for months. To no avail. He'd failed hard enough and often enough to finally admit his failings and do the one thing he'd never thought he would.

He had been forced to bring in help.

Luc padded into the small camp he'd created—the one he and his packmates used as a home base for their mission. Seeing as how each of his packbrothers had found his mate over the last few years, no one stayed with him for long. He didn't mind, though—caring for a new mating bond with time and attention was vital to a strong union. Or so he'd seen and heard from others over the course of his life. He had no firsthand knowledge.

"You should shift." Phego had already shifted human, had arrived at camp long before Luc had, shifting human and donning a wool cloak to keep his human skin warm in the chilly night air. "You've had a busy couple days tormenting those human hunters. Be human for a time and eat something with us."

The "us" being he and his mate—a tall, dark-skinned woman named Michaela who was likely smarter than all the Dire men put together. The woman was a doctor, had midwifed for Ariel—the mate of Dire Thaus—and had healing skills that would be invaluable should he ever actually locate the women he couldn't stop thinking about.

But Luc couldn't shift—couldn't relax enough to allow his human side to take control. He was stronger as a wolf. More in touch with his senses, too. He needed to stay on his paws in case something pinged across his mind about the women. He needed to stay ready.

If Luc were honest with himself, he also would have admitted that he didn't like being human in these woods.

The darkness of them, the sense of malaise that plagued the very air around him, weighed on his human side more than his wolf one. No, Luc didn't want to shift human. In fact, he hadn't for days. Maybe weeks. He couldn't tell anymore.

Phego sighed and looked to his mate, Luc's refusal to shift obviously worrying him. Michaela didn't say a word—simply retrieved a plate and pulled the lid off a large black pot. The scent of something that had been simmering all day exploded through the air, making his belly rumble and his wolf drool. Michaela had been cooking. He padded a single step closer, his muzzle nearly dancing as he took in every scent he could, as he deciphered what she'd made for dinner. The aroma was so rich, so thick and deep, that it practically coated the area around them. How had he not noticed that when he'd come trotting into camp? He knew the answer, though—he'd been too concerned with his search for the women, with his hopes of dismantling the pack of unhealthy wolves in the range. Too buried under emotions that weren't his. He'd been focused on anything but that which was right in front of him. What more had he been missing?

"Here you go," Michaela said as she set a full bowl of what looked like beef stew on a tree stump. "Eat something, or I'll hook up a stomach tube and force-feed you protein shakes."

Luc huffed, staring up at her. Releasing a soft growl into the quiet night to let her know how unhappy that would make him.

Michaela gave no shits, though. "Try me, Luc. I'm not afraid of you."

And with that, she strolled off to join her mate closer to the fire, plopping onto the bench next to him and snuggling into his side. Leaving Luc to the dark and his dinner. Not that he minded.

He ate quickly, enjoying the bites of tender meat in

his wolf form, even chomping on the carrots and potatoes. Michaela was a good cook, and she liked that particular chore. Said it appealed to the science side of her brain. Luc was simply grateful that she made sure to feed him when she was here.

Luc joined the couple after he'd finished his dinner, rubbing his fur along Michaela's legs before curling up at her feet. His big body taking up all the room between her and the fire. Thanking her the only way his wolf knew how to do.

Phego chuckled. "You're awfully soft on my mate, Alpha."

Luc couldn't argue that, though, to be honest, he was soft on all the mates the fates had gifted his pack. Omegas, the lot of them—powerful shewolves that were often seen as blessings in their world when they weren't being hunted and exploited for their gifts. He cared for all of them— Sariel, Amy, Charmaine, Ariel, Michaela, and Zoe. Each one brought heart and strength to their Dire Wolf pack. Each one a blessing upon the wolves he called brothers. He was soft on them because they deserved to be honored and respected as family and as amazing individuals. He'd stay soft on them, too.

The short night of late summer above the Arctic Circle fell deeper and darker in the forest, the air growing colder with every minute. Even in wolf form, he could feel the chill on the wind against his skin. If the pack were keeping the women in human form as a way to weaken their wolves—the only reason Luc could come up as an explanation for why he couldn't sense them—they'd be far more susceptible to the weather. Were they cold? Freezing, even? Did they need to be rescued? He'd do anything to save them, had given up months of his life just on the chance of finding them. If they needed him, he'd be there—once he got a bead on where they were.

"What if we never find them?" Michaela asked, almost as

if she'd been reading his mind. She snuggled closer to Phego, keeping her feet and ankles against Luc's side. Connecting the pack in her quiet way. "What if these women are not actually out there?"

Unthinkable. Something was out there—Luc could feel it. Sense it. There was no turning his back on the sensation, no avoiding the pull to do his job. Something or someone or multiple someones in these woods needed him, was calling on him to save them. He knew that down to the tips of his claws.

Michaela, though, wasn't finished exploring the path of her thoughts. "What if they're perfectly happy in this messed-up pack—"

Luc shifted on instinct, growling the entire way through the change. "They're not happy."

His sudden appearance and deep, throaty snarl did nothing to dissuade the Omega, though. "How do you know?"

"Because I can feel them." A lie...sort of. He could feel something calling to him—but not the shewolves in particular. Something that was impossible to explain to people who didn't even understand how much their own emotions weighed him down. How his sense of the world around him crushed him at times. He knew because he did...there was no better answer.

Michaela frowned, turning her attention back to the fire. "You sense the badness about this pack, I know—but what about the women do you feel? Are you sure it's them?"

He was not sure of anything anymore.

Phego cut into the conversation, leaning over his mate to look Luc in the eye. "Your obsession is concerning, Luc."

Of course it was, but that didn't mean Luc would stop. "The fear I can sense coming from these women—from within this pack—is more concerning. If you could feel it the way I do..."

But they couldn't. No one could. It was just Luc, alone with every emotion experienced by all the people for miles and miles bearing down on him. Just him and the gift that had been slowly driving him insane for centuries.

The mated pair looked to each other, speaking without words. Shutting him out, or so they thought. Luc could feel their disbelief, their worry. Could sense how much they doubted. He'd never been doubted by his pack—never had a brother question a single order he'd given or a plan he'd laid out. This was new, and Luc didn't like it.

He didn't want to stick around and suffer their disappointment for another minute. "I'm going for a walk."

Michaela rose to her feet, sending a jolt of concern punching through the air. "Are you sure? It doesn't seem safe out there."

Safety was an illusion, so Luc didn't answer—simply shifted to his wolf form and padded out of camp. Leaving the pair behind so he could dig for his own emotions once more, connect to his own feelings instead of everyone else's. There was a spot overlooking the lake that he liked to visit, one that brought him far more peace than he'd experienced in a while. He headed there practically on instinct, finding an outcropping to sit on so he could look over the vastness of the range before him. There was no such thing as quiet in his world—not with everyone else's emotions slipping inside his mind all the time—but sitting there, looking over the valley, was about as close as he'd ever come to it.

Bliss. This must be what bliss feels like.

But exhaustion was a bastard that creeped in uninvited, and Luc was definitely exhausted. Bone-tired. He'd spent so much time in these woods, so many days and weeks and months chasing this pack and looking for women he couldn't be sure existed. He should have surrendered, should have accepted that the women weren't there once he'd realized the pack contained no feminine energy. But they had once, or maybe his mind had played tricks on him. Maybe he'd been wrong that one time he'd sensed…something. It didn't matter, though. The fates wanted him right where he was and refused to allow him the strength to walk away. For reasons he'd never understand, leaving was impossible for him.

A fact that his fellow Dire Wolves worried over.

Something was very, very wrong in the Brooks Range, and that negative energy had infiltrated his family unit. The feeling was bigger than pack, though. It was quite literally everything. A shadow covering his entire world and darkening every inch of his soul. Life had gotten harder as he'd searched these woods, his senses growing stronger and his balance weakening. The so-called gift of intuition he'd used to his advantage for centuries had become more of a curse, draining him of his own feelings and leaving him empty. For the first time in over a millennium, he felt as if an end was coming. Perhaps his. Would he welcome the blessed silence of death? Or would he fight for every second on this rock? Would he surrender or battle through? He didn't know anymore, and that lack of passion for the very concept of life might have scared him more than anything ever had.

Which was why he clung to his mission. Why he refused to give up. Why his wolf wouldn't allow him to.

Over the last few years, Luc had assumed the tiredness that had started wearing on him had been eased by the Omegas who'd joined his pack. With each mating, he'd been given an infusion of energy, of strength. But even with Deus finally finding his witty and sarcastic Zoe, the added Omega energy wasn't enough to ease the aches in his bones. To control the power that threatened to bury him in other people's emotions on a daily basis. No, the Omegas weren't enough anymore. He needed something more.

He needed to find these women.

He needed to save them.

He needed that victory to keep going.

In the distance, a wolf howled a lamenting song, the soulful cry reaching for the heavens and dancing through the low spruces covering this part of the range. It took Luc a full ten seconds to fully recognize what that sound was, to sense it. To feel the energy of the pack. To understand that the entire unit was no longer stagnant.

The pack was on the move.

Everything within him perked up, tiredness gone. Senses on full alert. The pack—the living, breathing sickness of the range—was definitely in motion. Their energy cleared the static from his mind, recentering his world directly on them.

Time to go.

He was running toward the massive energy spike without thought, racing toward the sound that would lead him to the pack along the mossy ground. Unable to stop himself from following them. Not wanting to either.

Must find the women.

Two

*C*assiel had never expected to be in the herbal medicine business, but that was certainly how she had come to earn an income. Not that she needed much in the way of actual US dollars. Living in the Alaskan bush meant there wasn't a lot she had to buy—she participated in a barter system long ago worked out to cover the need for most things she might want, and she'd adjusted to going without most of what she couldn't get access to. Still, brewing essential oils and selling ointments and salves kept her coffee can lined in case she ever needed something nature couldn't provide her.

The copper still she'd scrapped together made a soft hissing sound as the lavender she grew was processed into oil. Dried flowers hung from the shed's ceiling, and various pots and containers rested along the windowsill and walls. If a stranger had walked into this space, Cassiel would have bet they'd think she was a witch brewing magical potions. Considering her Calendula ointment had been successfully used as an anti-inflammatory in the bush for years, maybe she was.

"What do you think, Moxie? Am I witchy to you?"

The little black-and-white Alaskan Husky, one of her six sled dogs, whined and jumped at her, begging for attention, which Cassiel happily gave. Her dogs and her little shed of plant healing—those two things fulfilled the deepest needs within her. She had fallen into both of them accidentally, but they had ended up being blessings in disguise. She loved her life, her dogs, and her job. But she especially loved sledding with her dogs out on the trail, whether in the blistering cold of winter, racing across the snow and ice on a sled mounted on runners, or in the excessive heat of full summer, her dogs still pulling her sled but with specialized wheels she'd found that could cover the rough terrain of the Boreal forests of the Arctic.

Perhaps mushing wasn't the most economical transportation method—her dogs could eat her out of house and home—but it was her favorite. Even in the summer months, when the ground grew thick with moss and the sun blazed down twenty-four seven, she loved strapping her dogs into her special sled with wheels instead of runners and taking them for a slow jog to Bettles. Her team may not have been made to withstand the heat of an Arctic summer, but they loved to run and she knew how to keep them from overheating. Besides, riding on her ATV or her snow machine wasn't nearly as much fun as standing on the runners of her little basket sled while the dogs raced along. Not to mention, engines broke and fuel cost money—the dogs were easier. She fed them, she took care of them, and they offered her transportation. Total win. She needed to be able to access the biweekly plane that brought supplies through the region, and getting to the landing strip in Bettles on foot was a hell she had no intention of experiencing. Dogs were better, especially the sweetheart little one she tended to treat more as a pet than a working dog.

Unable to resist the little whines for attention, Cassiel grabbed Moxie's face and gave her a couple good ear scratches. "Who needs a bunch of stuff when I have you guys, huh?"

No stuff and no people. Cassiel definitely didn't need other humans—she'd created a happy family with her sled dogs and knew enough of the people who lived in the bush to have interaction when she wanted it. The solitary lifestyle fit her just fine.

Cassiel looked over the still one last time, checking to make sure every drop of oil had been collected, before extinguishing the flame. The entire shed needed to cool down so the oil could be worked with, which meant it was time for her to head home. Still, she couldn't help but grin when she saw the amount of oil she'd processed. This would be a good batch, would make her lots of money once she put it into soaps and sprays, candles and roller tubes. And the Calendula teas and salves she planned to make this week would be another boon. Lots of money coming in but, more importantly, lots of items to trade with the locals for caribou meat and other supplies to help her and her dogs get through the upcoming winter.

"Come on, Moxie. Let's go home and make sure the rest of the dogs are settled in for the night." She checked one more gauge, verified the fire was completely out, then locked up the little shed just in case. If she put in another full day at the shed, she'd have a good supply of products to sell and trade the next time she met up with the supply plane. Her waiting list for Calendula salve was long and her cache was low on meat, but she'd been waiting for her blooms to flower completely. A few more days and they'd be dried and ready to process into the healing medicines the bush folk loved.

"Maybe I should use my money to buy the parts for a greenhouse. Then I could grow my plants more regularly than I do in the shed." Cassiel looked at Moxie, who seemed happy enough with the idea. "We'll talk to some people, see if anyone has an old greenhouse frame or knows where I can dig one up. Maybe even just a couple of windows to make a small one to start. I could connect it to the house so I can grow through the early parts of the winter."

The dog didn't answer, not that she expected her to, but that didn't matter to Cassiel. In fact, she rather liked not having to listen to others talk. The relative silence of the region had always been one of its biggest selling features for her. Relative because there was no such thing as silence in the forests—too many creatures and critters running around at all hours, especially during the never-ending sunlight of June and endless night in the depth of winter. And some of those critters were of the claw and teeth variety. The Brooks Range wasn't exactly overrun by predators, but it also wasn't the safest place to live. There were definitely scary creatures out there—big, mean animals who would think nothing of stripping the flesh from Cassiel's bones and eating her whole.

She'd grown accustomed to the threat of the beasts over the years—had plans in place and weapons to protect herself in case the black bears showed up or the lynx that roamed the tundra decided she was a threat to them—or a tasty treat. Living alone in this level of wilderness came with some pretty severe dangers, but she'd grown to understand them. To be prepared for them.

At least until the last few months.

As the seasons had turned from spring to summer—as the days had grown longer and eventually never-ending—she'd felt something in the woods closing in on her. Developed a sense of something wrong polluting her land. She couldn't quite wrap her head around what the threat constituted, though. What made it up. All she knew, all she could firmly grasp, was the unease that had plagued her lately. The dark energy swirling around the woods. She'd felt that sense of dread before, an uncomfortableness in her own skin that ate at her confidence. But lately, it had grown so much worse.

Which meant she needed to make it safely home before the darkness of the upcoming short night fell. "C'mon, Moxie. It's dinnertime for me anyway."

The two hurried to her little cabin sheltered against some tall spruce trees. The dogs—protected in their little day pen where they could run around but not get into any trouble—grew excited as their packmate rejoined them, though they yipped and cried more for Cassiel. She was the food giver after all. They'd already had their dinner, but she tossed a few extra bits of dried char fish their way to give them something to do while she put away the last of her supplies and readied her property for the night.

By the time she left the pen and headed for the cabin, Cassiel had all of her dogs following along beside her. Close—she wanted to keep them close. Night had finally fallen. The world had gone dark, not a single artificial light around. Nothing but the soft glow of moonlight sparkling along the lake in the distance and stars twinkling in the velvet above her.

"It's beautiful tonight, guys," Cassiel said, taking a moment to enjoy the cool air blowing down from the tundra. The worst of the summer was already over, the temperature dropping her into what she liked to call jacket weather. This was her favorite time of year—that little window before the days stayed below freezing and after the bright and deep heat of the summer. Just a month or so a year of blessed coolness before she and the dogs would be plunged back into cold and dark. This was the best time to be in the bush, carving out a living and sustaining herself with what the land provided her, because the land was giving. And dangerous. So very dangerous.

A rustling in the shorter spruces on the other side of the

pen reached her ears, and Cassiel's heart began to race. She had dawdled too long. Nighttime was for predators in this place, and though she wouldn't be searching them out, it wouldn't be unusual for them to find her. Usually, she gave them their space and they left her alone in hers, but being outside after dark was asking for trouble. And she didn't need to put herself and her dogs at risk.

"Let's go, my loves." She hurried onto the porch and opened her front door, holding it ajar, kissing the air for the dogs to follow her. "It's puppy pile time."

Six dogs loped into the house with Cassiel following closely. A little piece of calm falling back into place as she closed and locked the door. Home. Shelter. Safety. It wasn't much by most people's standards—a bed, a chair, a soft rug made from animal skins in front of the wood stove, a tiny kitchen in the back corner, and not much else—but it was exactly what she'd always wanted. It was all she needed.

"You kids already ate, so don't go begging for my dinner as I cook it." Cassiel washed her hands, tossing a glare at the dogs. They saw right through her, though. No way would she ever deny them food. Heck, they still should have been outside, snuggled in their kennels for warmth and sleeping away the Alaskan night. If she treated them as most mushers did, they wouldn't be allowed inside. She couldn't help but spoil them, though. Each and every night, she brought her dogs—all six of them—home with her and spent the time before bed giving them individualized attention. All but Gunner—that dog hated to be touched. Out of her team of six, he was the only one she left alone. He liked it that way, too. Preferring to be close but not requiring any more interaction than when she tugged his harness on him. Cassiel had once been that way— so deep inside her own head that the very thought of someone touching her sent her mind skittering to the darkest corners imaginable—so she could respect that.

Once Cassiel had cleaned up, she pulled out a fish she'd caught earlier in the day and heated up her pan on the propane burner. Cleaning fish had become second nature to her, so she made quick work of removing the skin and guts and filleting the meat. No need for anything more than that one fish. A quick, nutritious dinner was all she cared about—a little protein and fat to fuel her body through the night and into the morning. Nothing special.

When the fish was fully cooked and looking delicious, she sat on the chair with the dogs at her feet. Each one received a small piece of fish from her plate, though none of them begged. They simply sat and waited, knowing they'd get something. She knew better than to feed a dog from the table—or counter, as it were—but she couldn't help herself. The puppers were her babies, her family, and her only friends out there in the wild. Besides, she always had been a dog person, always felt more at home within a pack of furry animals than anywhere else. She liked to tell people that she must have been a dog in a former life, a thought that made her chuckle every time.

"Would you let me into your pack?" she asked, glancing over six sets of sharp eyes and pointy ears. "I think you would. I think you'd be just fine if I had four legs instead of two and fur instead of skin. Even you, Gunner."

The big gray dog huffed, staring back with his cold, flat eyes. Yeah, he'd accept her. Him simply sitting so close to her was enough to tell her he saw her as one of their own. The other dogs—her sweet Moxie, old man Bert, excited Clara, sneaky Rogue, and lazy Lox—had been much quicker to allow her into their little world. Especially Moxie—the tiny pup had basically jumped into Cassiel's arms as soon as she saw her.

Dinner eaten and dogs spoiled, Cassiel cleaned up her mess and readied the house for an easy morning. There was no staying up late or early morning alarm clocks in her world—you slept when you got tired and woke when you were rested. The dogs would make sure of the wake-up part better than any electronic device could, though. They were endlessly chipper and excited to be back outside in the mornings.

Knowing the darkness would only last for a handful of hours, Cassiel crawled into her bed, smiling as the telltale clicks and thumps of the dogs taking their places on the soft rug broke the silence. Once they had all settled, she laid her head on her pillow, ready to end one day and move toward another.

She was half asleep—right on that edge between awake and not even close, where she could no longer tell her dreams from her reality—when a call from her nightmares sounded through the range. A cry filled with hunger and cruelty, with deviousness and pain. One she hated above all others.

That sound was a wolf howling to the night sky, and nothing scared her more.

The second howl had the dogs whining, had her pulling the covers up tighter around her to fight the chill dancing along her spine. This wasn't another nightmare—there was a wolf howling on the range. But she wasn't alone—she had her six dogs with her. Animals with better hearing and senses than she could ever hope to have. No way would they allow a wolf anywhere near them without creating a cacophony of barking and whining. The wolf would pass—would go about its business in the woods. Would hopefully leave her and her dogs the hell alone.

And if not? Well, she had a couple guns close by that would help her eliminate the threat.

Danger. Wolves meant danger. And she wasn't about to allow them anywhere near her land.

Three

Luc had run all through the short night, searching out the wolf he'd heard howling, but to no avail. No matter how much he hunted, how wide he let his senses roam, no matter how much input he suffered under, the beast was not to be found.

Bones aching and paws bloody, he finally stopped moving as the sun began its ascent in the east. The lake before him sat crystalline and still, the water likely cold but beautiful. Fuck, he'd run to hell and back, ending up far closer to some tiny human town than where he should have been. He'd also led his packmates on that same wild goose chase—Phego and Michaela had followed him. He could sense them easily enough, but they weren't alone in his head. There were also humans, members of the local native tribe nearby, likely hunting the caribou that migrated across the tundra and Boreal forests of the region, and all of their emotions had been hitting him for hours. The buzz of other minds and souls creating chaos where he craved calm, the feeling of other people's noise scratching along his spine.

Needing a few seconds of peace and quiet, Luc took a moment to accept the others and simply be. To experience the emotional bombardment from people nearby and absorb it instead of trying to find a way to block it. To lose his own feelings. He stilled and let the world roll on without him involved as he looked over that clear, perfect lake. Observing and not participating. Coming to a stop mentally, physically, and emotionally. The lake soothed him as it always did, something about it calming the hell his mind could become.

It took him several minutes to unearth his own feelings and emotions from under the weight of everyone else's, but in the end, he found them. And he wasn't surprised.

Luc was tired.

Above all else, his soul felt weary. Not happy, not excited, not content, not sad—just tired. And not the sort of tired that would have meant he needed sleep—though he really did. This sensation went deeper—Luc felt exhausted all the way to his core. A thousand years was a long time to be alive, and dealing with empathic input for the whole of it only made things that much harder, especially as his ability had grown stronger over the centuries. He needed something to keep him going, to give him a reason to turn down the volume and live just in himself. Maybe that was what this search for the women was—a quest to keep his soul firmly planted on earth. A hunt for something that could help buffer him from the constant attacks. He couldn't tell anymore.

Phego and Michaela yipped, breaking the silence of the woods to let him know they were coming, not that he needed the warning. Their love for each other preceded them, and the noises of their trek along his scent trail were impossible to miss. They were far from their camp, though, and there was guilt in that fact. Luc had led them out here for nothing. Had brought them all the way to Alaska for this unsolvable quest.

Luc had failed them as an Alpha.

He should have sent them home—sent them all far from him. Kept his Dire brothers and their mates away from his unhappiness and constant struggles and disappointments of late. Alas, his brothers would never allow such behavior. They'd always given him his space, but no way would they let him simply disappear into the wild, never to return. They'd drag him back to Merriweather Fields first, to the president of the NALB. To the man they should be serving instead of babysitting a sick pack and coddling Luc on his journey into madness as he searched for what would likely turn up as nothing. For ghosts.

Instead of moving toward Phego and Michaela, Luc took to his paws and plodded over the hill and in the direction of the lake below. He'd never been the biggest fan of water, having always preferred the freedom of a good forest, but something about *this* lake called to him. The size of it, the clear, clean water, the mountain in the distance—this area was truly a national treasure and one he loved. The entire Arctic region had intrigued him for a number of years, which was how he'd ended up there in the first place. It wasn't the mountains or the wilderness that had sung to his soul, though—it had been the lakes. The inland waterways bustling with life. Cool waters that carved their way through the permafrost and refused to be quieted even once frozen over in the winter months. The water had always been a beacon for him, and yet this had been the closest he'd allowed himself to come to any lake since he'd arrived in the region. He couldn't fathom why.

He worked his way through a small copse of stubby spruce trees, slipping silently across the spongy, mossy ground. Ignoring the world around him and completely focused on the lake ahead. At least until a scent hit his nose, one he recognized but that felt completely out of place. Lavender. Calming, soothing, subtle lavender, which shouldn't have been growing anywhere near this part of the country.

Luc followed his nose, his pace quickening as other scents came out to play—roses, sage, Calendula. That last one sank him deep into his memories, picking at something from far too long ago to remember clearly yet too distinct to forget. His pack, his first pack when he'd been nothing but a pup, had practically worshiped the orange flowers. An old wolf with magic in her blood had dried them and made tea and ointments with the petals, a sort of early world pain reliever that he hadn't been able to find for a number of years. Someone was growing plants out here. But how?

Noisy humans forgotten, mind clear and on a new hunt, he followed the scents, wanting to know the who and how and why of growing those particular flowers and herbs. The how question was answered when he hit a patch of flat land with little spruce trees growing in the sunlight and discovered a structure. A very human structure. There was a shed in the wilderness, blooms of all kinds brightening the small windows on the sides as if some forest fairy had taken up residence there and figured out a way to grow her flowers in the harshest of environments.

Luc stared at those windows for several seconds, letting the colors and scents calm his spirit. He couldn't resist taking a peek, so he trotted closer and stretched his neck upward, looking inside the steamy windows. Flowers lined every wall, bottles and jars sitting on a far shelf, and something copper that looked like a small version of what moonshiners used to make alcohol rested on a table in the middle. This was no moonshine operation, though—this was a place of healing. He could sense it. He could feel—

"Shoo, beast."

Luc jumped and spun, nearly growling as a small woman rushed toward him. As fate sucker-punched him square in the gut when he finally saw the person who had somehow snuck up on him. Short with golden skin and dark hair, she sucked the air right out of the sky with her beauty, but it was her peaceful nature, the pure aura of calm around her, that truly set her apart from the rest.

Calm soul…but she looked terrified.

"Get out of here, wolf, before I have to shoot you."

Luc watched with amusement as the woman scampered closer. Brave little poppet. Something about her appealed to him, something in the way her emotions touched him felt less intrusive than most. Hell, he hadn't even realized she was coming, hadn't sensed her out in the woods. Not until she was already right up on him. That alone was enough of an oddity to incite his curiosity. But when she finally met his eyes, when she looked right into the depths of his very being, curiosity went flying into space as fate slammed into his heart.

A bond, a sense of essential connection—a need to be with her and her alone. And yet…

Not.

The woman stood completely motionless, staring back at him with an intensity that seared him from a distance. Not breaking eye contact. The emotions within her—fear, mostly, along with some anger and quite a bit of yearning— danced along his senses, tiptoeing their way into his mind. Not blasting him as he would have expected. His emotions were, for once, stronger than those of others and they were clear—he wanted the little woman.

There was just one problem he could see. The pull from her, the rebounding attraction he'd felt through others including his own brothers and their mates, wasn't there. But something was. Her feelings weren't clear, but his were.

He wanted to be with her, to befriend her. To care for her. All feelings he'd never experienced before. Especially not for—he sniffed, taking in her scent and verifying his assumption—a human.

But that felt wrong, calling her human. He sniffed again, pulling more of her scent even deeper into his lungs, not catching the notes of a wolf on her at all. And yet, again, there was something. A lupine whisper on the wind that didn't belong there. A shadow of a beast teasing the air around her. Was she truly human or something else? A shifter of a breed he couldn't place? A witch or a fairy, as he'd imagined? How was that even possible? All of his brothers had experienced bonds to females and found mates in Omega shewolves, strong creatures with a storied past and a legendary link to the Dires. If this woman was somehow supposed to be in his life, was to be bonded to him in some way, where was her wolf?

Unable to skip an investigation into the creature, he took a single step closer. That movement seemed to break the spell he'd put her under, though. Her eyes grew large, and her heartbeat raced loud enough for Luc to pick up the sound. He'd scared her…badly. Fuck.

The little woman turned and ran, staying in her human form. Not shifting as one of his kind likely would have done. Perhaps she really wasn't a shifter—wolfless, but not quite human.

Fascinating.

Luc followed at a slow clip, curiosity and a deep need to keep her in his sights winning him over. The woman owned dogs—a number of them. She must have used them for transportation as there were a couple small sleds under a roofed structure at the far side of the fenced enclosure where the dogs seemed to be huddling. Lots of fish, too—dried fish hung under another open building, the telltale lines of flesh hanging from poles along the roofline common in this part of the country. Likely food for the dogs, if he had to guess. She'd built quite the life in such a desolate and aggressive region. He was impressed.

At least until she disappeared into her cabin, only to come back out with a shotgun. That was the moment she went from oddity inflaming his curiosity to someone to get the fuck away from. Not because she had a gun—living alone in the wild, protection from all manner of beastly things seemed a necessity—but because she raised the thing and pointed it right at him.

"I am not losing my dogs to some wolf," she yelled, bringing the stock of the rifle to her shoulder. Aiming for him. "You'd better get off my land. Now."

Anger, fear—she didn't like him one bit. And still, he watched her. Wanting to know more about her and their connection, which didn't make sense. Something was wrong with whatever bond they had with each other. She wasn't shifting, not coming toward him, not even locking her gaze on his the way he would have expected had their union been prescribed by the fates. But there was more than that—more than a missing link where he would have expected something else. Her emotions brushed against him but never sank in, something he'd never experienced. He could feel the emotions of other people like punches to his gut, but hers were softer. Gentler. Almost a mystery. Something shrouded in secrecy and unable to penetrate his mind. He liked that. A lot.

But she couldn't have been his mate—he felt no mating haze or deep, soul-driven bond reverberating off her. He felt his connection to her, but even that seemed weaker than expected. Perhaps all these years of feeling everything from everyone had deadened his own barometer, had overrun his feelings and left him empty. Perhaps she was meant to be another's mate, not his.

A thought that had his hackles rising and his growl building.

Fine—she was his. But maybe, just maybe, the fates had been wrong. He was definitely hers, but perhaps she wasn't his.

A one-sided mating? Just what he likely deserved.

But her lack of desire for him was really clear. And if the gun she continued to point at him was any indication, she certainly didn't seem to be falling into any sort of haze of love. In fact, she seemed to want to kill him.

"I'm not kidding." The woman pointed the gun in the air and fired once, making his ears practically bleed at the noise. "Get out of here, you giant mutt."

Mutt? What the hell?

Unable to let this go without knowing what he'd just encountered, he took a step forward. She did not seem impressed with that decision.

"Don't you even try it."

Luc never had been good at following orders. He took a few more steps in her direction, keeping his head low. Holding in the growl he wanted to release so as not to scare her any more than he already was. Her dogs began to bark and whine, growling at him from behind the wall of wire. The noise grating to his ears.

The woman stayed in a human form through all of it. Stayed mad, too, and she never let that gun drop even an inch. "You're not the first wolf to come up here and try to take out my dogs, and you won't be the last. But unless you want to be buried in the same field those other ones are in, I'd suggest you move on out of here."

Dead wolves. He was suddenly very aware that Phego and Michaela were close. Too close. This woman—this little wisp of a creature who felt very animal to him but wasn't shifting—was already uncomfortable with his presence alone. Adding two more might push her over some sort of edge of reason, and he wouldn't risk his packmates on something as frivolous as his curiosity. He would have to figure her out another day.

Knowing it was time to go, Luc dropped his head even more. Showing his submission for the first time in too many years to count. He was the dominant wolf in any situation, and yet there he was. Creeping away from her like some sort of scared, fluffy forest creature. Ensuring his head sat lower than hers to make her comfortable. He wasn't even sure she was a shifter—had no idea if she understood his actions— and yet he kept on. At least until he'd crept back enough to have coverage in the larger spruce trees, then he turned and ran away. Moving farther from the silence of her soul even as his wolf wanted nothing more than to stay beside her. A confusing emotional situation for sure.

It took him longer than he would have liked to meet up with Phego and Michaela, mostly because he kept stopping to look back over the lake, to try to pinpoint where that little cabin had been. The shed with the flowers. The dogs. The woman who'd somehow burrowed into his psyche. So yes, too long to meet up with his packmates, but not long at all to shift so he could address them in his human form once he had them close enough.

"There's a problem."

Phego shifted human, looking ready to kill. "What kind of problem?"

"There's a woman in the woods."

For a long moment, there was a stillness among the three shifters. The type brought upon by the inability to find the words one wanted to speak.

Michaela shifted from her wolf form, breaking that silence. "You found the women?"

"No. She's not one of them. She's…" He shook his head, seeking words he was certain didn't exist in the many languages he'd learned over the years and coming up empty. "She grows flowers."

They both looked at him as if he'd lost his mind. There was no time to accommodate their assumptions, though. He had a job to do, one that had just gotten harder. And more urgent.

Luc needed more backup than the two wolves could offer him. "Call in the rest of the team."

"What?" Phego asked. "Why?"

Because he needed more time to determine what his attraction to the woman meant. He also liked the quietness of her emotions on him—the softness. He'd been under attack from everyone else's presence for centuries—she certainly seemed like a nice change of pace. But devoting time to her meant he had to finish his job there. Meant he needed to cure the region of the sickness.

"Because I'm done hunting these fuckers. We need to find the two women and destroy the pack, and I want all hands on deck to do that."

Michaela looked almost horrified. "But the babies…"

The babies. The pups. Thaus' mate, Ariel, had given birth to the first child of the Dire pack, and Levi's mate, Amy, was pregnant with the second. Dragging them up here would put those tiny lives in danger, something he couldn't force them to do.

"Ariel and Amy can decide if they want to come."

Phego glanced at his mate. "I'll call Levi—"

"No." Luc stepped closer to his brother, his snarl pronounced. The order clear as the image of that tiny woman with her gun to her shoulder popped into his head. She wouldn't have wanted him to tell her what to do. He somehow knew that with a certainty that refused to be cowed. "Call the women first. Give them the chance to decide before their mate can make the decision for them."

Phego stared back at him, not breaking. A growing sense of unease wafting off him. "Thaus and Levi won't like this."

Yeah, Luc knew that, but he didn't give their dislike more than a single thought. Instead, he recalled his journey through the woods and how he'd felt the pull toward that lake, the woman with the gun appearing as if he'd somehow called her from the heavens. She lived there alone from what he could tell and had an obvious backbone of steel, along with a strong distaste for his wolf. She made her own decisions, and he would expect all of the Omega sisters to do the same.

"I don't care if our brothers don't like it," Luc said, his voice strong. His mind made up. "The women of this pack can and should decide their own fate."

A picture of the woman standing and pointing a gun at him invaded his mind once more, making his blood run hotter. Making his determination that much more solid. She would never allow someone else to choose her fate for her—he believed that all the way to his bones. And Luc wouldn't take the choice away from someone like her. Someone with strength in their heart and fire in their soul. Hell, he'd walked away from her—had left her there in the woods all alone after just finding her. Had probably turned his back on the mate the fates had thrown in his path. Maybe. Possibly. At least, from his side of the bond.

He'd left her behind because she was strong and independent and didn't need him or fate itself to make her choices for her.

Much like his Omega packmates.

What was she?

Four

Cassiel powered through her morning routine, not stopping for a moment once she walked outside. She couldn't—if she hesitated, the fear would come back. No, not fear. Anxiety. She'd been living under the low-level buzz of anxiety since the day that beast—that wolf—had come padding out of the forest like some sort of wraith and thrown her life into upset. That energy—that tingly feeling that made her want to run back inside and lock her doors all the time—pissed her right off. She refused to be afraid of the life she'd built, of the world she lived in. She would not give in to the phobia that had plagued her since she'd been that little girl in a group home looking out over the wilderness of Denali. She did not want to live in the nightmares she'd always had about the animals that seemed to haunt her. To hunt her.

For as much as she loved her dogs, wolves had always been something she avoided.

When the morning tasks were completed, Cassiel

grabbed the ganglines and harnesses, and started hooking up the dogs to her summer sled. It was going to be a relatively warm day, which would make the run to Bettles a little tough on her furry engine, but she only had one shot this month to trade her products and pick up her orders. She could have taken her ATV and ridden there, but the idea of leaving her dogs behind where she couldn't watch over them terrified her. No way was that happening, so sled it was. She'd simply have to leave with plenty of time and let them trot their way there instead of full running.

"Come on, Moxie. Let's put you in the swing spot." The little black-and-white Husky jumped and whined, so excited to be getting on the trail. Running was what these dogs loved; it was what they were meant to do. They'd run all day and night if she let them, not that she would. She wasn't one of those mushers who chained the dogs outside and ran them thousands of miles a season. Her dogs were her pets first, her transportation second.

Dogs in place, sled loaded with jars and tubes of her handmade medicinals, Cassiel grabbed the ganglines that connected to the harnesses, held on to the back of her sled basket, and began to push.

"Hike," she hollered, using the language she'd been taught by other mushers in the bush. "Let's go, dogs."

A solid push, a good scramble as the dogs found their footing, and they were off, racing along the path they'd cut through the spruce trees over the years. The wind on her face cleared much of the last few days' stress away, and she found herself smiling and relaxing into the ride. No worries about wolves or predators, no thinking about what could go wrong as the midnight sun of summer retired and fall came back to Alaska. She let everything go and enjoyed the ride. That was what she loved—time in the wild with her family of sled dogs. That was all she needed.

The mush to Bettles didn't take long at all—not nearly enough running for her or the dogs to feel tired—and the team arrived with time to spare before the bush plane landed. Cassiel found a shady spot, piled a little bit of dried grass for the dogs to lie on, and gave each of them a rubdown and a decent snack. Once the dogs were taken care of and resting, she got to work, organizing her shipments and readying a few boxes in case any of the tourists coming in for their fishing, hunting, and hiking adventures wanted to purchase from her. Most of her items were purchased by the local tribes and the people who worked the adventure fishing and hunting businesses, but quite a few were also shipped to other bush communities, picked up by the pilot and dropped off along his regular stops.

She had four boxes for the plane with her, all filled with tinctures and essential oils to help her neighbors heal their small scrapes and burns, their allergic reactions and skin afflictions. Those boxes would bring her food for the dogs and supplies for her own kitchen eventually, maybe even gasoline or oil for her snow and four-wheeling machines. She never set a firm price with her bush neighbors—simply trusted in the honor of the folk that they'd send her what they thought was fair for what she sent them.

The plane was also how she received the few things she needed that she couldn't grow or hunt, and she was expecting a good load of food—a couple blocks of cheese, flour and yeast to make bread, sugar and spices. All luxuries in her world, and totally worth the wait.

The low hum of the approaching plane growing to a roar as it dipped low enough to touch down didn't even bother the dogs, though that didn't surprise Cassiel. She'd been making this trek with them since they'd each been a pup. They were used to the noise. They even slept through the squeal of the brakes and the pilot—an older gentleman named Frank who claimed to have flown missions in the Vietnam war—hopping off.

"Good to see you, Miss Cassiel," Frank said with a tip of his baseball hat. "What do you have for me today?"

"Four boxes going on down the line. The stops are listed on the tops."

Frank nodded, likely knowing Cassiel always sent her shipments in an organized fashion. "I've got a couple notes for you from my last stop—you may have another order or two. I'll go ahead and start loading while you look them over." He handed Cassiel two sealed envelopes. "There's plenty of room for your boxes. I only had a couple passengers this time, and this is the end of the line for both."

Cassiel opened the envelopes and read over the notes, grabbing a couple bottles from her sled and wrapping the paper orders around them. She took a pen from her pocket and wrote the names and stops on them, knowing Frank would make sure they arrived safely even if they weren't boxed. Once ready, she worked with Frank to load her products, helping him organize the weight so the shipments would be easier to hand off at the stops and keep his plane balanced. Once done, he pulled her supplies from another compartment.

There weren't a lot of them, something that disappointed Cassiel. "No dog food?"

Frank shook his head. "The seller in Fairbanks said there were slow downs at the docks, and some of the freight forwarders were stuck waiting to unload. Do you want me to contact someone for you? See if I can get another plane up here?"

"No, it's okay. The weather's likely to hold for another few weeks, so I can make the run over every two weeks instead of monthly. The dogs will like the exercise."

"Those critters just like being with you, Cassiel. They

adore their human momma." He handed her one last small box. "A present from my daughter. That ginger tincture you sent her has really helped with the nausea."

Cassiel took the jar with a smile, already knowing what would be under the fabric wrapping. Frank's family ran an apiary that supplied bees to larger farmers in the lower part of the state. His wife and daughters sold and traded the honey they harvested from the hives, which Cassiel had been lucky enough to get her hands on a few times. When Frank had mentioned his pregnant daughter was having trouble with severe morning sickness, she'd known her ginger tincture might help her and had offered the family a bottle. She had to admit, she'd hoped to get some honey in return but hadn't asked for or expected it. That jar would be a treat.

"Thank her for me, please. This is a true gift and completely unnecessary."

"You are the gift. That cream with the yellow flowers has done wonders for the wife as well—her eczema's almost all cleared at this point."

"Well, you make sure she knows I'll always have more for her. Just let me know when she starts running low, so I can bring it out here."

"I will. And you enjoy that—it was a good harvest this year." Frank shook her hand and left to close up the storage compartments, leaving Cassiel to load her sled with the few boxes she'd received. A whine from her dogs caught her attention, though, making her stand to look over her surroundings. The dogs seemed on edge, something that rarely happened in town unless there was something in the woods to worry about.

Which there likely could be.

"Come on, pups," she said, rubbing each head in turn to grab their attention. "It's about time to go home."

But before she could get her team on the trail, a man

stepped around the side of the plane and right into her path. Someone she didn't know. He carried a huge rucksack that looked as if it could hold a person's whole life in it and was dressed like someone who understood the bush. The man looked prepared for his trek, unlike some of the touristy hikers she'd run into through the years. Not an unusual sight in these parts, and yet…

As she looked him over, something inside her pinged. Something that made her heart jump and her breath come faster, something that reminded her far too much of fear. That feeling plucked at a memory, and a certainty grew within her. She knew the guy, and yet she was positive she'd never met him. Tall, huge really, with long legs, light eyes, and a mop of wild, shaggy hair—he was too handsome to forget, too striking to ignore. He had a cruel sort of beauty, an air of danger and harshness about him. One that she liked. A lot. In fact, she couldn't take her eyes off him.

When he noticed her looking, she nodded, trying hard to not seem too forward as she asked, "You don't look like someone who hired out a fishing tour."

His face stayed stoic, his pale, blue eyes locked on what seemed like her chin in a way that felt oddly predatory. "Likely because I'm not. Bettles was just the closest town to where I need to be."

That fit the region for sure. The range didn't have a lot of what one might call towns. Or roads. "Where are you headed?"

"I'm camping out at an old, abandoned homestead on the far side of the lake there, so I'm angling that way."

Cassiel knew the basic location of the place—she'd seen it on her flights in and out of Bettles over the years. A good chunk of flat land with five, maybe six cabins and a decent structure used as a drying rack and for storage. She was pretty sure no one had lived there for years, though it seemed as if that was about to change. Perhaps only temporarily. "Big place and far enough to need more than your feet for transportation. That's a multi-day hike."

"Two days from here, I figure." He shrugged, still not looking directly at her but acting totally casual. Calm. Seemingly confident in his abilities.

Cassiel didn't feel calm or confident, though. All she could think about was the wolf—the huge beast that had walked up on her the other day. Two days alone and unprotected in the wild with predators like that could end badly for the man. Something she did her best to stop thinking about.

Something she failed at. Completely.

"On foot and with the land as sloppy as it is in the summer, plus all the bugs? It'll likely be more like a three-day hike for you."

Needing a moment to collect her thoughts, she fiddled with the ganglines and verified that her dogs were paying attention and ready to go, then she did the neighborly thing. What any good bushman would do.

"I'm mushing out in that direction. I can take you to my land, which will put you most of the way to yours if you like, but there's no way I can take you all the way. There's no trail around the far side of the lake, and this isn't the weather to make my dogs forge one. They'll overheat."

He looked at the dogs, suddenly seeming uneasy. No longer calm. "You want me to ride that little sled. With the *dogs* pulling us."

The way he said the word dogs—with a bit of a judgmental sneer—knocked neighborly right out of her vocabulary.

"No one said you had to take me up on my offer." She turned and grabbed the back of the sled, ready to make a running start to the ride home, but he stopped her.

"Wait, please," he said, coming up behind her with

quick strides and solid footfalls. "I'm sorry. I'm just not used to this mode of transportation. Dogs make me...nervous."

She patted the seat of the sled and gave him her best smile. "Well then, hop in and prepare to be amazed."

He took his time loading himself into the sled, not that Cassiel could blame him. The man was large—tall and muscular, with long legs that had to be folded just so for him to fit in the seat. She was not tall and had always been in the musher's position on the runners. She'd never really thought about the comfort of a rider because she'd never had one. Her basket sled wasn't really built for a rider—it was more of a sprinter's sled than a distance one—but the dogs could handle the weight if she was careful about her pacing. They'd pulled more for longer, just not another human being. How could they? She'd been their only passenger for...well, Moxie was coming up on seven, and since before her so...

A long darn time.

Had she really been alone all those years?

Not the time to think about this.

Once the man was settled, Cassiel pushed the sled to a start and hollered to the dogs. "Hike. Hike!"

This time, she let the dogs run however hard they wanted, let them pick up a little speed on the way home. She couldn't help herself—the faster they went, the more expressive the man became. In fact, as the dogs hit a solid gallop, he had slid into a full-blown panic. With every turn, he grabbed the slide of the basket as if afraid they'd tip or crash, which made Cassiel laugh. He definitely did not laugh.

"Are you sure this thing's safe?" he asked for the fourth time as they rounded a particularly sharp turn.

"Oh, sure. We only crash once or twice a year." She chuckled as he gripped the sides of the sled once more, his knuckles white with the pressure of his hold. Cassiel enjoyed having this man in her sled—he was fun. And easy to make uncomfortable.

As the dogs slowed around a massive rock formation that marked the trail to her property, Cassiel took advantage of the quieter moment to be polite. "I'm Cassiel, by the way. And I live right up ahead if you end up needing anything. I figure I'll be your neighbor for your stay here. What's your name, stranger? And how long are you planning on living at the homestead?"

The man looked over his shoulder, his eyes nearly silver and so much like those of her dogs that she almost slipped right off the runner. That look, that meeting of their gazes, sent something spinning inside her. Punched her square in the stomach and left her breathless. And hot. So very hot.

"I'm Luc, and I'm here until I get a particular job done."

*F*ive

*T*he ride through the woods pleased Luc more than he'd thought possible. It could have been that the constant internal pressure, the static of other people's presence and feelings, quieted when he was around Cassiel. That stillness in and of itself he considered a gift. But really, his enjoyment came from more than just the silence. The peace he felt around Cassiel originated from a deeper place, one he couldn't quite grasp. One he didn't know how to access. There was a wall around her that he would eventually like to break through, but for now, the silence in his mind that she seemed to bring with her was lovely.

The dogs settled into their run well, though they'd been a little antsy when he'd walked up. Nervous, likely sensing the predator in their midst. But once Cassiel had mounted the sled and started them moving? They were excited but steady, doing the job they obviously enjoyed doing. He was almost jealous of them—he wanted to be running, too.

"How far will they go?" he yelled to Cassiel as he stared out at the dogs.

"Much farther than we need to. I used to race them for fun, and they ran twenty hours straight one time."

"That's a long run."

"They loved every second. Trust me, if the dogs don't want to run, this sled isn't going anywhere. These babies were born and bred to do exactly what they're doing, and they enjoy it."

"Even in the heat?"

"Yeah, though they'll tire more quickly because of it. Still, this sled on wheels is far better for both them and me than any vehicle with an engine I could buy."

Luc settled against the seat a little more, allowing himself to relax and enjoy the ride. The dogs were happy, enjoying their exercise, and obviously ignoring the wolf in the sled. Smart beasts. The woman…well, he was still trying to figure her out. He couldn't look directly at her without his wolf pushing forward, without feeling some sort of tug drawing him to her. The sensation, the need, was almost blocked by her. As was her scent, which was far weaker than he'd ever experienced. He couldn't tell the reason for the subtlety or if the lack of her essence could be related to something else, something more personal. Something he didn't even know how to begin to heal.

He might not have the knowledge to take care of whatever was holding her back, but he had a plan to find out how. One he'd initiated the moment he'd stepped onto the grassy landing strip two stops down from the town of Bettles. When he had paid the pilot to take him to the tiny town on the edge of some national forests where hunters and fishermen paid people to show them around. Cassiel's town.

The sled ride to Cassiel's plot of land took a number of hours, something that irritated Luc's inner wolf to no end. He hated to be so still. He wanted to be running with the dogs, racing them, but that wasn't possible. Not unless he wanted to give up his secret as not just a wolf shifter but an ancient breed of one. Dire Wolves like him—stronger, meaner, bigger than standard wolves—were supposed to be extinct. There was only his pack left that he knew of, though Phego's brother had shown up a while back claiming more had created a pack in Australia. The man had been a bit insane, to be honest—trying to kill Phego for some slight he'd been obsessed about. Still, whether there were his seven or more, wolf shifters never expected to see one.

If Cassiel was a shifter of some sort, she could know the history of his breed. And she likely was some sort of shifter— she had to be. The idea of her being human and him still feeling such a strong bond with her didn't sit right—Dires bonded with Omega wolves. At least, his pack certainly did. Not one Dire Wolf had found their mate in a human. He was certain about the whole mating thing with Cassiel. They had a connection that defied reason, so if she wasn't truly a shifter, perhaps she had something about her that his wolf wanted. He had no idea what that could be, but he'd find out. The woman was a puzzle to him, and he loved puzzles.

Eventually, they pulled to a stop close to the little camp where he'd first seen the spry woman, where he'd first felt the pull to be close to her. Luc looked it over with new eyes as Cassiel slowed the dogs to a stop. The pen for the dogs, the dry fish hanging inside an open-sided but roofed structure, the cabin with the wide porch. Everything neat and tidy, unlike some of the bush homesteads he'd come across. Living off the grid the way she did lent itself to eccentricities and hoarding things one might need, so a bush plot ended up looking like slapped-together junkyards sometimes. Hers looked like a proper home. Cassiel was obviously resourceful and independent, strong enough to live in the harsh conditions this area of the state brought upon her. She impressed him immensely.

"This is your place?"

Cassiel nodded as she untied a couple of the dogs. "Yep. All mine."

She led the released dogs to the pen on the side of the house, giving them lots of head scratches and affection. She even cooed to some as if they were children who could understand her words. The dogs, meanwhile, chattered away with her, wagging tails and jumping up for more of her touches. They absolutely adored her, and she obviously felt the same for them.

Luc couldn't look away, fascinated by their behavior. Wolves and dogs didn't usually mix. The lesser animals sensed the greater predator and avoided them. But Cassiel's…they were all over her. Another strike against her being a wolf shifter.

Or maybe they were just well trained. Luc needed to figure that part out…and he could. "Can I help?"

"Sure. Grab a dog."

He looked over the last couple, his wolf wary as their beady eyes followed him. Watched him. Every one of them seemed just as nervous as he'd expected them to be and not at all as excited as the ones Cassiel was still dealing with.

"I know how you feel," he whispered as he approached one little beast. Black and white with long ears, the dog didn't even reach his knee height. Thankfully, instead of biting him when Luc reached for the ropes attaching her harness to the sled, she rolled over and showed her belly. Luc…well, he petted it. Because what else could he do?

"Good girl. Come on now. Let's get you where you belong."

One tug, and the dog hopped to her feet, following at his side. Unlike the ones Cassiel took to the pen, this little female didn't whine or whimper; she didn't bark or yap. She definitely didn't wag her tail either. She walked with her head down and her tail tucked between her legs as if terrified Luc would hurt her. That fear made things inside him loosen, made him want to do something to appear less threatening to the creature. He had no idea what that might be, though. He'd scared people for centuries, had likely given Cassiel a bit of a heart attack the first time she saw him when he had been in his wolf form—holding back on his Luc-ness simply wasn't something he'd ever even tried.

Once he led the dog to the pen, Cassiel took over, loving her all over and letting the little beast hop around before she took off the harness that had been wrapped around the dog's chest.

Before Cassiel could close the gate that would keep the dogs from running off into the woods, the little dog hurried back over to him. Finally calm and happy, she rubbed her side against his leg, looking up at him and wagging her tail.

Cute little thing.

"Well, thank you, miss." He patted her head, watching in fascination as she practically melted into him, as her tail sped up and she grew brave enough to seem to want to crawl into his lap. He knelt before her just in case that was exactly what she wanted. "Not so scared of me after all, are you?"

Apparently not, because she climbed right into his lap and looked back at Cassiel. The woman shook her head and laughed.

"You are such a needy little thing."

"So, it's not just my charm and witty personality?" Luc patted the dog's head and scratched her ears, grinning when she moaned and leaned into him. "Ah, I see. It's the head scratches."

"That and bacon in your pocket will win them over every time."

"Noted. Okay, girl. Time to get up."

The dog yipped and jumped up for one more face lick before running off into the pen. Cassiel closed the gate and organized the harnesses in her hands, watching over her animals. Such a normal, everyday sort of moment—a woman caring for her pets. Luc was almost envious of the simplicity of it.

And yet there was more work to be done. Places to go and things to investigate that couldn't be done at Cassiel's, which meant he needed to finish up helping her unhook the dogs. Reluctantly, he stood and headed for the sled once more, his confidence buoyed. His mission firmly plotted in his head. His objective clear.

And yet, he had to look back at the pen just one more time. Had to see if the little black-and-white dog stood staring back at him.

She was, and that fact warmed his cranky, old heart.

Dogs and wolves getting along…who knew?

Each taking one more dog, Luc and Cassiel moved the last two from sled to pen, patting heads and wincing as their barks grew more crazed, more excited.

Okay. He may have been the only one wincing.

"They're ready for dinner," Cassiel said, smiling broadly, her tanned skin glowing from the cold and the exertion. "A good run always ramps up their appetite."

"It certainly seems that way. Are they your only transportation?"

"No—I have a four-wheeler and a snow machine, but I don't use them often. Engines break and need gas. These guys are easier and serve multiple purposes."

"Like what?"

She ticked them off on her fingers. "Transportation, companionship, they're my friends, my hunting partners, heating blankets in a pinch, and a really good alarm system. That's all I can come up with off the top of my head."

But one word had been enough to make Luc cock his head as he asked, "You consider them friends?"

"Of course. I know it's not always what's done with sled dogs, but they're family to me. Besides, I only have the six to pull my sleds. It's not like I have a huge team of forty or fifty dogs to deal with."

True—most sledders had much larger packs. "Well, whatever you're doing seems to be working. They definitely like you."

"They do. They're my world out here." She sighed and looked out toward the lake, her energy changing in the blink of an eye. Calming visibly. "The camp you need to get to is just over that ridge. It's a good day's hike, though. And sunset will be on us in about another hour or so."

Luc was not good with human interactions and non-direct language—he preferred to be assertive and say what he meant. So, he did. "You want me to stay here for the night."

She seemed positively taken aback. "No."

Luc frowned, looking out over the lake. Trying to find firmer ground between them. "Then I should hike out now?"

"That's a bad idea."

Two options, both refused. Cassiel was an enigma to him. "I'm not sure what else I can propose."

"Are you always this structured?"

"Yes." He made the mistake of looking directly at her, and his wolf surged forward. Those eyes, that face, the aura of a forceful sort of peace around her—there was something about Cassiel that he couldn't ignore. Something he and his wolf found desirable. And yet still, the pull to be closer had no rebound, a situation he'd ever known to happen with shifters. It wasn't all-consuming like a mating bond at all. There was no haze of need to fight through, no impossible-to-ignore desire for touch and taste and sex. There was just him and her and her dogs standing in the middle of the Alaskan bush. But he didn't want to leave.

Cassiel finally blinked, breaking the long stare they'd

endured. Her face flushing even more than the cold had caused. "Well…I need to feed the dogs. If you absolutely must hike out there tonight, you'd better get to it." She bit her lip, not meeting his eyes. Fidgeting with the edges of her thick coat. "But if you'd like to stay, I've got room in the house for a pallet on the floor. I can offer you that and some reindeer stew." She swung that dark gaze around, stabbing him with a hard look. "That's it, though."

Her *it* sounded amazing, and though he never should have accepted her offer, he was hard-pressed to decline. "I'd appreciate the hospitality, and I promise to be on my best behavior."

"Well then, come on. Let's get these dogs fed and the sled put up for the night before the monsters start creeping out of the dark."

"Monsters?"

She kept moving, casually tossing back a single word.

"Wolves."

Luc's lungs froze up, his gait hitching slightly before he caught himself. Wolves…like him. And definitely not like her. But she didn't know about his inner beast, didn't have an understanding of what he could do on two legs and four paws.

So he stayed casual and calm…and only moderately disappointed that she'd called him a monster. "You see a lot of wolves up this way?"

"Sometimes—depends on the weather and the migration patterns of the prey animals around here. There's a lot of predators up this way, though. Wolves, black bears, lynx, even wolverines sometimes—all things you don't want to run into alone, unarmed, and in the dark."

Luc followed her, his brain spinning.

A woman terrified of wolves—their bond was something unknown and impossible to build on. What was he doing there?

And why did he feel as if leaving was the worst decision he could make?

Six

*C*assiel had absolutely no idea what she was doing other than leading her life into certain ruin. She'd invited this strange man to stay, welcomed him into her home when she knew next to nothing about him. When she had been alone for so very long and liked it. She didn't need a man hanging around and bothering her, not even one as handsome as this Luc character. He may have drawn her eyes more than once on the ride back to her homestead, but that didn't mean anything more than he looked good. Looks could be deceiving. Trusting in something so fleeting and disingenuous to tell you anything about the person? That was…

"Stupid." She hissed the word as she walked toward the drying rack, hoping like hell the noises from the dogs covered her.

Luc turned toward her, though—looking up at her with those killer light-blue eyes. "What's stupid?"

Cassiel had failed. Miserably. Might as well be honest at that point. "I'm stupid."

"For what?"

She grabbed the cart she used to lug the dried Arctic char

to the dogs and tugged it deeper into the storage building for fish flake. "For asking you to stay, of course."

Luc's eyes grew wide and his mouth opened, but it took him a solid few seconds to be able to find those things called words. "I can assure you, you're safe with me. I would never harm you."

The laugh that exploded out of Cassiel would likely have insulted a certain number of men, especially those she'd met in the bush over the last few years. The ones who thought power came from control and a woman like her shouldn't have been out in the wild alone. Might as well make sure Blue Eyes over there wasn't one of them. "Luc, I've lived alone in the wild for most of my life. I trust this heathen land to take care of me far more than I do the promises of men like you. Besides, I'm armed to the teeth. I'm not worried about you hurting me."

"Then why are you stupid for asking me to stay?"

"Because…" She dragged a number of fish into the cart, moving swiftly through the rows and grabbing the dried meat in a pattern that was likely only in her head. Concentrating and letting the words and the truth fall by the wayside.

But Luc, while helpful as he took over controlling the cart so she could focus on fish selection, was not one to settle for silence. "Because why?"

Cassiel stopped, spinning, pursing her lips and bringing her hands to her hips. She'd had a foster parent call that her Peter Pan stance. She certainly didn't feel like him right then. "I like my solitary life, Luc. I like my patterns and habits, like knowing what needs to be done and handling it on my schedule. I know there are people who can't stand being alone so much, but I enjoy it. I love this little world I've built." She waved her hand at him, frowning harder. "And you'll mess it all up."

His grin spread slowly, creeping up his face to those

eyes that made her breath catch. Looking at her in a way that weakened her knees and her arguments. "I'll mess up everything—this entire world you've created—in just one night?"

"It could happen." She huffed, tossing one last fish into the cart before leading the way outside. "Fine. I'll stop worrying about you Godzilla-ing my life here. Just don't go thinking you can drink all my coffee."

He followed her, pushing the cart. Sounding far too pleased with himself as he said, "I would never."

Her doubt was high, though. As was her anxiety. No, Cassiel didn't fear Luc would try to harm her. She trusted her gut when it came to people, and her gut told her he wasn't the type to take advantage. Her fear came from her own reaction to him—she liked him. Wanted to know more about him. Wanted to crawl all over him and feel him just to find out what his touch was like.

Cassiel had never been so attracted to another human being before, and that desire threw her slightly off her usual steady course. And yet, he was only there for the night. Just one. He had his own homestead to build, it seemed, his own life to live. She was likely worrying over nothing.

Luc dragged the cart across the path to the dog pen, veering off to the side where she had chains hooked to the posts, pausing every time she reached inside the cart to pick a fish. Large buckets of rainwater sat along the path, and she ladled some liquid into the bowls with the fish at each post to help soften them up a bit and to make sure her dogs were hydrated. Soon enough, it would be too cold for the water to sit like that. Then, she'd be adding hot water she'd boiled instead to make them a soup in the morning. Maybe some kibble as well. Their dietary needs depended on how much they'd worked, and today had been a good workout for them. They would need the extra fat and protein in the fish to stay strong and healthy. Needed to drink the water with the fish in it to replenish what they'd burned off. Tomorrow, she'd feed them a little bone broth to increase their collagen and protect their joints. Anything to make their life that much better.

Her dogs might as well have been her children for how much she cared for them, how she worried about their health and safety. She loved the furry little beasts, and anything she could do to make them happy was worth the struggle. Including lugging around gallons of hot water in the winter.

"Do they stay out here?" Luc asked as the dogs ate their dinner.

"No. Most mushers do leave the dogs outside at night, but I prefer to bring them inside. It's a small team."

"It's a small cabin, too."

She would never have argued that point. "We manage just fine."

Once the dogs were fed, Cassiel walked with Luc to the building she used to dry her fish so they could store the cart, then led him back to the pens. Unable or unwilling to leave his side. Especially as the shadows began to lengthen and deepen in color. It was time to head in for the night for sure. The sky had darkened to a degree that made her neck itch, and she was done being out in the gloom. Without leads or harnesses, she released the dogs from their feeding chains, slapping her hands together and watching them run around a little before whistling for them to come home. They responded immediately, racing onto the porch. Settling in a line to one side of the front door with their tails wagging and their ears cocked. They were ready.

"Stay," she ordered before heading off to the wood pile to grab a few extra logs for the fire. Not for herself—she preferred to sleep in the chill of the summer nights. Besides, her dogs kept her warm. But Luc...well, he was Luc and likely not used to living the way she did.

As Cassiel completed her tasks, Luc stayed beside her. He didn't push her, didn't rush her or question her chores. He simply followed her around, making sure to jump in when he could, staying out of her way when he couldn't. He carried the logs back to the porch—an unnecessary and yet appreciated gesture—following her straight to the entrance of her little home.

No time like the present.

The dogs rushed inside when she opened the door, their fight to be first pulling a subtle chuckle from her guest as the remaining dogs trotted behind them. Once inside the house, though, Luc's confident demeanor shifted. He suddenly seemed uncomfortable. He also dwarfed the place, Cassiel observed as she padded to her tiny kitchen to put on the kettle to boil some water. Perhaps that was why his eyes couldn't hold still, darting along from point to point as if trying to take in every detail of her place.

It wasn't until she opened the refrigerator that he even seemed to take a breath.

"You have electricity?"

She patted the old Kenmore model she'd paid a small fortune to have brought up to Bettles. She'd even had to borrow a larger sled and a few dogs from the local tribe to bring it to her cabin. Worth it, though. "Solar power. I tried to use the river that runs behind my place for hydroelectric, but the distance was a bit too much. I upgraded to solar a couple years ago. I also have a backup generator and a decent supply of fuel just in case. I don't really need it except for in the summer months—no one, not even the dogs, wants to eat rotting fish."

He nodded, still looking around. Still absorbing all the pieces of her life. Her trinkets and drawings, books and blankets. All the things she considered so very personal, suddenly on display to a stranger. She couldn't watch him any longer, so she moved to prepare their dinner instead. Trying to ignore him. Fighting not to feel the weight of his eyes on her as they continued to move.

He's just a man.

"So, the drying rack outside?"

"I have friends who bring me salmon. I dry that and the char I catch out there and then smoke them for feeding the dogs in the winter. We get a great breeze here, so I can dry fish all summer long."

"But you bring some inside."

"If the wind stops or it gets too hot. Last month, I kept everything I caught inside because we were up in the eighties during the day. Now that we won't break fifty again, it's all outside."

But it was when she turned on the faucet to wash her hands that he grew positively incredulous. "Indoor plumbing."

A man who was obviously surprised by such things as an actual toilet and sink. "Of course I have indoor plumbing. The toilet is one that composts, so there's no line to run or sewer to deal with, and the water is mostly rainwater."

"You're ingenious."

"No, I'm a woman who grew up in homes with these things and who doesn't want to live without them if I don't have to. Just because I live in the wild doesn't mean I want to camp out every single night of my life." She stared out the window, the darkness making her want to shrink away from the fragile glass. The shadows so very deep and dark, menacing. "Besides, it's best not to be outdoors once night falls. You'd be smart to heed that warning."

Luc stepped closer, taking up every inch of room, it seemed. Goodness, the man was *huge*. "Because of the wolves."

She swallowed hard, trying like hell to keep her hands from shaking as she put a pot of stew on the burner to warm. "Wolves, bears, wolverines...all manners of predators up here."

"Why do you stay?"

She shrugged, stirring. Focusing on the stew because looking at him had become far too difficult. "I like the peace and quiet."

Luc stood silent for a long time, the only sound coming from him the whisper of his breath. At least until he said, "You like living alone."

A statement, not a question. One that flicked at sore places inside her because she knew where this particular thought process might go. And as she had no interest in traversing those dark and dangerous roads once more, she kept her answer clipped. Vague. "I'm used to it."

"And your family?"

A harder flick, one that almost made her twitch. "Never had one."

He quieted again, his breath growing hushed. Softer. The sound soothing the anxiety building within her. Lord, when had she gotten so sensitive? She never had been one to talk about her past, but she'd long ago come to grips with it. Luc asking her a simple question shouldn't have rocked her world the way it had. Shouldn't have made that age-old hurt resurface. Something about him, about his presence in her space, set her on edge and made all her emotions escalate. That had to be it. She just had to get him to stop asking personal questions, had to redirect the conversation to something safer for her. Something that wasn't all sorts of screwed up. Something—

"Will the dogs be okay with me taking up some of their space? I'd hate to make them uncomfortable."

And there he went, retreating to a topic that put her firmly back on solid ground. Surprising the hell out of her, too. "Oh, sure. They'll be fine. They might puppy pile on you at some point in the middle of the night, though."

"I'll be prepared."

"Good." She looked up finally, meeting his gaze. Giving him a grin. "I care about my dogs more than most humans, so I'm glad you already know your place. Now, how about you set a couple of those bowls on the table? This stew will be done in just a few minutes."

He did as he was asked, heading to wash his own hands in the little bathroom first. Giving her enough room to take a deep breath. Dinner, clean, sleep, and then he could go. Could stop filling her space with his handsome face and those eyes that stabbed her straight in the heart. Could take his manly self right back out into the wild where he belonged. And he did belong there—she could sense it. Feel the wild within him. Luc was no more a city person than she was. He had the wilderness in his soul, just like her.

Which only drew her to him more.

Seven

Cassiel confounded Luc at every turn. There were things about her that definitely spoke to him, that called to his wolf in a primal sort of way, but she was a human. At least, it certainly seemed that way to him. Mostly. The more time he spent with her, the more he questioned it. In her home, with all her things, he could smell wolf on her, but only barely. The scent weak and whisper-thin. And there was no sense of lupine spirit around her or within her. No feel of the energy of the wolf to grasp. There was just her, alone in her little cabin with her dogs. Looking so very beautiful to him.

But as he stared at the woman who'd taken him in for the night, the only wolves he could sense were those who made up his own pack. The Dires and Omegas were definitely on their way to the camp around the lake, close enough for him to feel not just their energy but their emotional state. He could sense their excitement and worry, some anger, too. He had a feeling he was going to pay for bringing them up here, particularly with Thaus and Levi. Not that he could blame them. Still, the women deserved the chance to make their own decisions. The rest of the pack would need to work to keep them all safe. He'd make sure they did.

But first…

"I don't have a couch," Cassiel said as she stacked furs and blankets on the floor. "And my bed's only a twin, so there's no room for two."

He'd make room to share a bed with her if she invited him in, not that he could tell her that. "The floor will be fine."

"Are you sure? I can sleep on the floor, and you can take the bed. It'll be a spell before you can get a mattress up to that homestead."

Luc caught her eye, loving the way her neck flushed with blood when she looked at him, the way her heart skipped a beat loudly enough for him to hear. "This is perfect. Thank you for your hospitality, Cassiel."

The dark-haired angel nodded and hurried into the bathroom, snagging some clothes along the way. Likely to change. To strip the cloth from her flesh and be naked and natural. Luc wished to be able to join her, to investigate every inch. To scent up and down her body and see if he could wake up whatever was calling so loudly for him. He kept his spot on the floor, though. Removing the layers he needed to and keeping himself as covered as he believed Cassiel would deem appropriate. He preferred being naked—always—but he had a feeling she would kick him out for that, and he was desperate to stay. To figure her out.

So, his clothing remained. Mostly.

"All yours," Cassiel said as she walked back into the room, the clothes she'd been wearing folded in her hands, her long black hair obviously brushed and shining in the dim light of the room. So pretty, this girl. So sensual without even trying. She crawled onto her little bed in the corner and grabbed what looked like a journal, writing down words Luc couldn't read from where he sat. Ones that weren't his business.

He rose to his feet and headed for the little bathroom,

needing a moment to pull his head together. To refocus on why he was there—to scope out her place, figure out what his attraction was to her, and settle his wolf. Nothing more, nothing less.

Luc relieved himself and washed up for the night, rejoining Cassiel in the main room. She looked half asleep, curled up under blankets in the dark with her eyes hooded and her breaths quiet. She wasn't, though. He could sense her awareness of him—her body responding to his when he moved closer. Not too close, though. He wasn't going to join her in her bed unless she asked him to. He simply needed to make it to his own without tripping over one of the canines scattered across the floor.

Once he had traversed the obstacle course known as Cassiel's cabin, he settled into his pallet bed, still keeping an eye on the woman across the way. Needing one more point of contact before he allowed his body to rest. "Goodnight, Cassiel. Thank you again for allowing me to stay."

"Goodnight, Luc," she said, her voice breathy and quiet. "And you're welcome—come by any time."

He hoped to take her up on that.

With night fallen and the lights out in the cabin, the dark of the wilderness crept inside. Blackness was a true thing in the bush—no lights anywhere unless the moon hung bright and thick. They were in the waning, though, so even the moonlight seemed cut off and weak. The shadows grew darker and more luscious instead, taking shape and gaining weight to them as the minutes passed. And still, Luc waited. Sat and listened and bided his time until he was sure Cassiel was in deep sleep.

And then he crawled off his makeshift bed.

Luc would have liked to have said his curiosity with the woman was purely situational—it wasn't every day he ran into a female living alone in the bush. He knew better, though. His wolf was attracted, his human side definitely so as well. And while he'd never hurt her, never do anything to her that would be crossing her personal boundaries, he knew what he was about to do was close. Close enough to make him need to sneak.

He crept to the side of the bed, then leaned closer. Not touching her—that would be a gross violation of her trust—but sniffing. Scenting her. Allowing his beast to come forward and letting his senses unfurl from the cage he kept them in most days.

Weakness. That was his first impression and one that unsettled him. Cassiel was anything but weak. But the more he sniffed, the more that feeling became pervasive. The more he sensed how deep that scent had been buried. It wasn't Cassiel who was the weak one—it was something inside of her. There was a beast within her, one who'd never been given the chance to develop properly. One who was dying slowly—oh, so slowly—inside the human form.

Wolf. That was the lupine scent around her, the feeling of connection between them. She was a wolf shifter after all, though not a strong one. His own wolf whined inside him, wanting to call to what he knew to be another wolf in need. Wanting to care for the poor animal that had suddenly become pack to him. Wanting to howl for her, to give his strength to her. Luc was not one to disobey the wolf spirit within him, which meant they had work to do.

He crept back across the darkened cabin, slipping under the blankets Cassiel had provided him and staring across the room in her direction. Pack. He had a definite sense of pack with her. That could explain why he'd not been able to stay away, why he'd felt such a strong urge to bond with her. He'd gotten lucky finding those cabins around the lake and had taken that luck into his own hands by climbing onto the bush plane in the hope that she'd be at the stop in Bettles.

A risk that had definitely paid off, though that success had brought more confusion with it. More uncertainty.

What was he going to do about Cassiel and her dying wolf? The need to keep her safe had grown exponentially while he'd been in her presence, which meant he needed to change his plans. Staying close to her had suddenly become a priority in his head, and finding ways to take care of her was right behind it. He and his team had an obligation to deal with the women of the Brooks Range pack, the ones he'd been hunting for so long, but Cassiel needed him, too. If the local pack caught wind of her, if they ever found her and figured out her secret, she'd be in as much danger as the other two. She was a commodity, something others would see as valuable property to control. She was in danger from more than just the local predators. She just didn't know it.

But Luc did, and the very idea that anyone could try to harm the little woman was abhorrent to him.

His responsibilities seemed to be growing both massively and quickly, multiplying right in front of his eyes, but he'd manage. He'd have to. His wolf would never let him give up on a member of his own pack, and somehow, Cassiel had become just that. His to watch over.

A Dire Wolf not of blood but of soul.

⸻

Sunlight bathed the little cabin in the morning, pulling Luc from his slumber. He'd slept well, better than he had in a year at least. Of course, he hadn't lived indoors very much over that time, preferring to stay in the wild in his wolf form. Even just a stack of blankets on the floor had felt like a luxury to him, and he was grateful to the little dark-haired female for the opportunity to rest. The one moving about the kitchen and obviously trying to keep from waking him. The one whose inner wolf now sang to his own, her lupine scent obvious and mouthwatering.

It was time to get up.

"Morning," he grumbled, rising to his feet. She turned, and her eyes automatically panned over his body, her cheeks flushing when she stopped at his bare chest.

"Morning." She brought her eyes back to his for just a moment—just long enough for his wolf to lunge forward in his mind—then jerked away as if embarrassed she'd been caught looking. He liked the feel of her eyes on him, though. The heat that flared in the dark depths of them. The attraction he could feel from deep within her body. Clothes? Not needed. Hell, if he hadn't been worried about her feelings on the matter, he would have slept naked. Shifters preferred not to be burdened with such things.

Humans, on the other hand…

"I'm going to make us some breakfast before my morning chores." Cassiel took her attention away from him and returned it to the food before her. "Figured you'd need something in your belly for the long hike ahead of you as well."

Yes. Because he had to leave her behind. At least for now. "Thank you. Breakfast would be much appreciated."

"No problem." She continued to cook—fish, toast, and eggs, it smelled like—so Luc took the time to redress himself and spend a few moments in the bathroom. Hands and face washed, teeth brushed to clear away the dryness in his mouth, he headed back out to the main room. To Cassiel. Whom he would be forced to walk away from in a few hours. That did not sit well with him or his wolf.

"Come," Cassiel said when she spotted him, smiling his way and beckoning. "Eat with me."

The light shone in from a window behind her, and her smile enhanced the glow. She was an angel with a heavenly name. And he was unable to resist her. He was not about to deny her anything.

Breakfast passed as meals tended to between two people feeling each other out—with light conversation, gratefulness on the part of Luc for Cassiel gifting him such a meal, and polite denials from Cassiel when Luc claimed that had been the best meal he'd had in years.

"It's just fish and eggs."

"And toast." Luc held up the browned piece of bread, something he knew had to be almost a luxury in the bush. "Don't forget the toast."

"Fine." She handed him the last dish to wash—because no way was he making her cook and clean up—before moving to wipe down the table. "And toast. It still can't be the best meal you've had in years."

He shrugged, drying the plate before placing it on the shelf where it belonged. "I've been out in the wilderness for a long time, and most of that I've spent alone. So yeah…it was the best." He glanced outside, the yipping of the dogs catching his attention. "They're outside?"

"Yeah, I let them out so they could run around a little."

"Not in their pen." Luc spotted three of the six little beasties chasing one another through the tall grasses. "They won't run off?"

She huffed a laugh. "They know where the food is and have no intention of leaving it behind."

Smart dogs. "Can I help you feed them before I go?"

Cassiel shook her head, her smile falling. Her eyes darker. "That's not necessary. You'd better get on the trail if you want to make it to your homestead at a decent hour."

Because she thought there were things in the woods more predatory than he could be. An idea he could play along with…for the moment. "Can't be out after dark."

"Right."

Too bad she had no idea that he was likely the most dangerous thing in the bush. Him and his pack…which he needed to meet up with. He had responsibilities, ones that would take him away from her. But he'd be back. He had no doubt about that.

"I'll just be on the other side of the lake," he said, tugging his backpack into place. "If you need anything, I'm more than willing to help."

"And I'll just be on this side of the lake. In case *you* need anything, seeing as how you're the newbie up here and all."

Damn, he liked that sass. "Very true. I'll probably need something. You should expect visits."

Her neck flushed, and she dropped her gaze to the ground. "That'd be fine. You're always welcome on my land."

Fine, indeed.

Luc wanted to stay so badly, to help Cassiel with the dogs and keep learning about her. To give her wolf time to adjust to the presence of his and see if he could somehow reach the poor, weak creature. But he had to walk away from the little cabin and the pretty, dark-haired woman, had to hike into the woods on the pretense of a two-legged trek around the lake. He had to begin his journey to the homestead on the other side because his pack would soon be there. He could feel the anticipation, anger, and love radiating from his packmates as they converged on the far northern area of the Brooks Range—a veritable buffet of emotions spilling out into the world and zooming toward him across the distance, creating a sort of static in his mind. One that didn't bother him as much as the sort that came from strangers. His pack—his family—would soon be there to help him deal with the local pack. And oddly enough, he couldn't wait to see them all.

Though, he still wished Cassiel could come with him. Hidden wolf spirit, dogs, and all.

Eight

Three days. That was how long it took until Luc showed up at Cassiel's door again, not that she had missed him on those long, lonely days and nights. Not that she had been happy to see him.

Not that she wasn't exceptionally skilled at lying to herself.

"Hey there, stranger." She tugged her ponytail a little tighter, hoping the wind hadn't made her cheeks too red. "How goes the homestead?"

Luc—every tall, thick, muscled inch of him—strolled out of the woods as if he hadn't just walked what must have been eight hours to get to her. And he looked so darn happy to see her.

"Good afternoon, sweet Cassiel. The homestead is coming along, but I wanted to see you." He held out a bag, smiling her way. "I wanted to repay you for your hospitality. I wasn't sure what you needed, but I figured gauze, tape, and antibiotics are pretty standard fare for anyone living up this way."

He wasn't kidding. Cassiel took the bag from him, not even considering turning it down out of politeness. Medical supplies were hard to come by. "This is amazing. You really didn't have to do this, but thank you."

"I know I didn't have to—I wanted to. And you're welcome."

Cassiel stood there, grinning up at him, unable to look away from those light eyes. Unable to move—at least until the dogs began to yip. She shook her head a little and laughed.

"Sorry. I was just…" *Daydreaming? Zoning out? Thinking we should get naked?* None of those felt like good answers.

Thankfully, Luc didn't seem in a hurry for her to finish her sentence. "Yeah, me too." He reached out and wrapped his fingers around her elbow, still smiling, his movements slow and not at all threatening.

But something wasn't quite right. "You look tired. Are you feeling okay?"

He sighed, that smile finally falling. "I've had…a headache. For a few days."

"Oh, like a migraine?"

"Similar, yes," he said, sounding slightly wary.

Cassiel nodded. "I knew a girl once who got those. They really made her sick. Is there anything I can do to help?"

"Just me being here is already helping." He tugged on the handles of the bag he'd brought her. "How about you put this up, then I can help you with whatever chores you were about to do?"

"I was actually about to make lunch. Would you like to join me?"

"I wouldn't want to impose," he said, but his eyes belied his words.

Cassiel couldn't hold back her grin. "Yes, you would. You'd impose all over the place for more of my homemade bread."

"Guilty. I miss bread sometimes out in the wild."

"You should get some yeast and flour. You don't need

anything else. Well, salt. Yeast, flour, and salt, a good Dutch oven, and a fire. There you go."

Luc followed her inside, ducking through the doorway. "I'd likely just make a big, soupy mess. You'd have to show me what to do with that yeast, flour, and salt."

"I could do that, though my bread takes a full day to rise. You'd need to be here overnight again."

She caught the implication behind her words—the hint at another sleepover—and sucked in a breath. Was that too forward? Would he assume she meant more than sleeping on her floor? Would he—

"If you offered the invitation, I would stay again. Your floor was quite comfortable."

Awkwardness, aborted. "Then we'll make a plan for that. Are sandwiches okay?"

"You're just teasing me with more bread."

She laughed. "Maybe."

They sat together at her wobbly little table, him dwarfing his side. He really was quite large—unusually so—not that Cassiel much cared. He was handsome in a cruel and harsh sort of way, but kind and not at all scary to her, even though he had to be three times her size. The man moved as if comfortable with his height, though. As if he understood people might be nervous about him. No quick jerks or sudden stops—he moved with a fluidity that defied his size and showed more natural grace than Cassiel had ever seen in another person. She loved to watch him maneuver her world.

She really just loved watching him.

After lunch, Luc joined her to tidy up the dog pen, though how he got any work done, she had no idea. Every time she glanced up, his eyes were on her, his body angled in her direction. Not that she minded. He looked at her in a way that made something go molten inside her, made her body tingle in ways she was not accustomed to. She couldn't decide if she wanted to drag him to her bed or kick him off her land. More than likely the first option, which brought with it loads of issues and possible complications. Best to keep her hands to herself.

"So," she started as they moved to put away her tools in her shed. "What are you doing up here anyway?"

Luc stretched past her to hold open the door, handing her a pitchfork as she ducked past him. "Research."

That seemed awfully...vague. "What kind of research?"

"Biological. Examining and investigating the region's animal populations and diversity."

"That sounds..." *like way more than she could ever do seeing as how she never actually went to school* "...hard."

Luc's lips ticked up in what she considered a smile, though it didn't quite reach his eyes. "I watch animals do what they do all day, tracking the sick ones to see how their illness affects the rest of the population. It's not hard at all."

"Oh." Yeah, it still sounded like more than she'd know how to do. "You don't look like a biologist."

"I don't?"

"No. You look like..." *like sex, like desire, like a runway model* "...you should be on TV."

He laughed and turned away, seeming embarrassed by what she could only assume sounded like a compliment. Sweet Luc.

"The dogs look good."

Subject change, accepted. "They do. I've been letting them rest a little bit more than usual, but we're going on a run tomorrow."

That caught Luc's attention. "Where will you be mushing to?"

"Just across the valley and around the far forest. It's not a rough path, but it'll take almost all day to do the loop, especially with the weather so warm." Not that Cassiel thought forty-five degrees should be considered warm, but when you were bred for snow and wore a thick fur coat, air temperature became something to worry about.

"And the dogs can run that far?"

"That much and farther. They love to run." She slipped past Moxie, patting the beauty on the head and leading Luc toward her cabin. "These dogs were made to run—they were bred for it. I need to keep them happy, and running makes them happy."

Luc looked over her dogs, following her onto her porch. "They certainly seem happy."

Cassiel took a seat on one of the chairs she'd salvaged from a dumpster one of the few times she'd gone into a larger city. It had taken her days to bring them back, the bulk and weight slowing her down considerably, but she loved them. They were definitely a luxury item and one she rarely got to use, but the day had warmed nicely, and the house was blocking the worst of the wind. Sitting on the porch with her new friend seemed like the most perfect thing to do.

Luc must have agreed with her because he took the chair next to hers and settled in, looking out over her land. Staring off at the lake in the distance.

"What other runs do you normally do?" he asked.

"We run all over the land here. We've mushed all the way to the oil field along the ice road in the winter—which, even in Alaska, brought a lot of attention our way."

He steeled her with his light gaze, his lips lifting into a smile again. "I bet you just loved that."

Sarcasm…she was fluent in it. "Totally. Fifteen people staring as if you were some sort of sideshow act? It's every girl's dream."

Luc chuckled, settling deeper into his chair. "So, you giving me rides to the oil fields is pretty much out of the picture?"

"You would be correct. I want to be nice, but you can take a hike on out there yourself. Or hop on one of the supply planes that comes to Bettles."

"They come through there often?"

"Every other week, just like clockwork. At least, the bush plane. The stuff for the oil fields will start coming in once the ice road forms across the Jim River."

"And you meet the bush plane every time?"

"No, but usually once a month, for sure. For picking up supplies and for trading my wares."

That definitely piqued his attention. "What do you trade?"

"Herbal remedies."

He sat back, looking at her in what she could only describe as shock. "You make medicine?"

"Yep. Soaps and salves and ointments to help others in the bush with the most common of maladies."

"Like a doctor."

It was her turn to laugh. "Goodness, no. I didn't even go to high school—I'm no doctor. I'm just a girl who pays attention when people way smarter than I am tell me stuff. There are lots of plants that can fight things like skin irritations and inflammation just as good as the drugs we don't have easy access to, but it's hard in this climate. I grow them in a shed that is surprisingly warm, process them into usable products, and sell those. Simple."

Luc leaned forward, resting his elbows on his knees as he stared straight into her soul. "Cassiel, you are anything but simple."

Her heart jumped, her body warming under his gaze. Who was this man, and why did he affect her so? Why was she so drawn to him? And why did he look at her as if he felt the same sort of way—attracted?

But then he stopped looking, his head whipping toward

the lake as if he'd heard something. His face hardening for a moment before her sweet, calm Luc returned. But his smile didn't.

"I should get back before it gets too dark." He sighed and gave her what she could only describe as a sad sort of look. "Wouldn't want to run into any predators on their nightly hunts out there."

She didn't know what had just happened, but she wasn't going to try to force him to stay if he wanted to leave. It was already late enough that she wouldn't have started the trek around the lake, but Luc seemed set on leaving. Or perhaps he was sad to say goodbye.

She preferred that thought.

Cassiel followed Luc off the porch, watching silently as he hoisted his hiking pack onto his back. Crossing her arms over her chest as he finally turned as if to say goodbye. Saying the only words she could in that moment.

"Thank you for your help and your company today. Stay safe, Luc."

"You too, Cassiel." His eyes burned into hers, calling something from deep within her toward the surface. Making her skin itch and her blood run hot. What was it with this man? Never before had she reacted to anyone that way, just Luc. Her huge, muscular, light-eyed neighbor.

The one who had his own homestead to get back to.

Luc nodded once before turning and walking away, leaving her alone with her dogs once more. Cassiel watched him go, unable not to follow him with her eyes. A heavy sort of sadness entering her chest once he disappeared through the trees.

"Ridiculous," she finally said to herself before spinning on her heel and heading back to the house. She needed to get some work done—check on her still and put up some fire cider so it would be ready to sell in the fall. Already, the days were getting shorter and the nights colder. Summer would be over soon enough, and she'd be fighting off the Arctic cold. So much work to do before then.

That night, Cassiel sat on her porch once more, this time alone and in the dark. She'd been unnerved all evening because of Luc and his quick departure, but her unease was more than that. Something in the air, something she couldn't explain, had made her anxious. Had been pinging at her survival instincts all evening. Her dogs seemed calm as ever, though, so it couldn't be something in the woods.

And yet, as she sat in the dark, she felt watched. Hunted, even. But Moxie and her crew lay at her feet, mostly sleeping. No barking or whining, no ears up and focus locked on something Cassiel couldn't see. They were completely at ease while she fretted.

"You are losing your mind," she said to herself before grabbing her blanket and heading inside. The dogs followed as usual, rushing toward their favorite spots for sleeping. Her protectors completely calm and ready for bed. She needed to relax.

And yet, for the first time since she'd moved in, she engaged the lock on the door before walking farther into the cabin to get ready for bed. Double-checked that the rifle she kept in the little table she used as a nightstand was loaded, too.

No sense courting trouble and all that.

Nine

*H*unting for days on end left Luc tired and frustrated. In the past—before his pack had started sending members to the region to assist him—he'd have curled up under a tree and napped away his ire. He couldn't do that any longer. He also couldn't avoid his homestead because it was no longer just one or two members he needed to spend his time with. His entire pack had finally arrived.

The chaos in his mind from all of the input of his pack descending had worn on him, so he'd held off going back to the cabins Phego and Michaela had worked hard to set up for the group. They'd turned eight abandoned structures into proper homes, ones he had barely spent any time in, choosing instead to sleep in the woods halfway between his homestead and Cassiel's. He was grateful for all the work and for his pack to join him on this mission, but the constant static in his head grew with every day, every hour, and every mile lessened between them. He just wanted silence, which was why he'd broken down and headed back to Cassiel's that morning. He had craved her peaceful soul and needed the quiet being around her brought his mind. She silenced the world for him, which was quite the feat.

As Luc raced back to the cabins where he could sense the final members of his pack had arrived, he wished for more time with Cassiel and her quiet mind. More mornings of breakfast and warm smiles, of taking care of the dogs and her kind words. He needed her brightness, craved the safe harbor of her little cabin in the woods. He also wanted to keep her safe from what was coming. What was out in the woods and on the range, far too close to her for his liking. His attention was split between his pack, the women he needed to find, and Cassiel. The pressure from all sides felt enormous.

Luc had left Cassiel behind this past time with nothing much more than a see you later, falling prey to the darkness permeating the area the farther he'd moved away from her. Cassiel's light, her pure heart and clear emotions, couldn't penetrate the bleakness, but they had definitely held it back while he'd spent time with her. The farther he'd moved, though, the less he'd felt that peace. The less he sensed her as well. It had been days since the last whisper of her spirit had joined his, which was why he'd gone to see her. He'd been anxious over thoughts of her alone in the woods, and that anxiety seemed to only amp up now that he had to leave her behind a second time.

Soon, he told his wolf. *We'll come back to her soon.*

Luc hated the thought of soon because he knew it would never be soon enough.

"The prodigal son returns." Deus stood on the porch with his mate, Zoe, as Luc took the final steps onto their land. The two radiated love, a warmth that drifted through the home and the land around them. His pack was a happy one, a full one, with him being the only unmated member left. The loneliness of that fact was not lost on him.

Still, he shifted and threw on the cloak Deus tossed him, coming to grab his brother's forearm in a traditional greeting. "Good to see you again, brother."

"And you." Deus nodded to Zoe. "She's going to take you inside to meet the others."

Suddenly the two standing outside to greet him seemed more like a wall between him and those inside the house. As if they needed protecting...from him. "Do I suddenly require a chaperone to meet with my pack?"

Zoe stared him right in the eye, something few wolves could do. "Ariel is here."

Ariel—mate of Thaus—and a woman of intense emotions who broke Luc's heart at every turn. Luc had felt the low thrum of the vortex inside of her since his brother had found his mate in the brave Omega, but it was stronger there. More chaotic. Fear and stress and anguish permeated Luc's Alpha bond to her, and he didn't want to exacerbate that. She'd been a victim of a ring of kidnappers who'd held her hostage and run experiments on her. Had tried to breed her forcibly. She carried the scars of that time both on her body and in her mind. Luc would never want her to think of him on the same level as those animals. So if Zoe was planning to run interference to keep Ariel calm, he would accept that.

Luc nodded to Zoe. "Lead the way."

He followed the Omega inside, bathing himself in the pure happiness of the space. Ignoring any of the darker, sickly sensations coming from outside in the world. His pack all together created almost a bubble of emotion so strong, he didn't think he'd ever experienced anything like it. He loved that sensation. Such a stark contrast to what he'd been feeling in the forest and in the days leading up to this reunion.

It reminded him of being with Cassiel.

"Luc," Thaus called, standing slightly in front of a small, dark-haired woman who could only be his mate. A woman whose eyes couldn't meet Luc's but who stood tall and strong—shaking but holding her ground. Such a brave little wolf.

"Peace, brother. I mean no harm." Luc stepped closer, keeping his own emotions reined in so as not to influence the Omega. Watching her carefully in case she spooked. "You must be Omega Ariel."

The woman nodded, reaching out a hand even as she kept her arm locked with Thaus'. "Nice to meet you, sir."

The chuckle Luc let loose came all the way from his belly. "There are no sirs here, sweet Ariel. We are family, and I am so happy to finally meet such a vital part of ours. You are as strong as I'd expected you to be."

Zoe and Charmaine—Mammon's gorgeous blond mate with a heart bigger than the mountains around them—appeared at Ariel's side, both women looking positively fierce. Ready to protect their sister at all costs. Such strong women to have been brought to his pack—gifts from the fates, truly. He couldn't help but wonder how Cassiel would fit into this group. If she would.

"Would you like to meet the baby?" Michaela appeared from a hallway, carrying a blanketed bundle that had his wolf sitting up and taking notice. A baby gave off no sense of male or female, of gendered energy. The only thing he could sense from within those white blankets was love and security, the purity of a new soul that he rarely ever got to experience.

Ariel spun, a smile breaking across her face as her son neared. The overpowering, endless love between mother and child was something Luc could have stayed wrapped in all day, but Thaus eclipsed even the strength of that with an emotion so deep and fierce, Luc couldn't even imagine walking around feeling that all day. His brother adored his little family and would absolutely, no doubt, murder anyone who dared to put them in danger.

He would be an amazing father for the little pup.

Ariel took the baby from Michaela, bouncing him a few

SAVAGE SALVATION • 83

times before turning back to Luc. Before pulling all of her emotions together and giving him a stiff smile.

"This is Micah." She glanced up at Thaus. "Our son."

Pride. So much pride filled the room. This was the next generation of Dire Wolf, the continuation of their ancient and legendary line. Another time around the circle of life for their pack. The very concept staggered Luc.

"I am honored to be in your presence, sweet Micah. Let your Alpha take a look." He took the baby from Ariel, being careful not to make contact with the skittish wolf and holding the child in one hand. Once the child was settled in his grasp, he shot Thaus a look. "An angel name for a Dire Wolf."

Thaus grunted. "We figured one generation of demons was quite enough."

Indeed. "It is a strong and noble name and will suit him well." Luc leaned down, letting his wolf come forward. Sniffing all over the child to permeate his scent in Luc's memory. Eventually, Micah's masculine energy would develop, but for the moment, he was all love and light—the pure innocence of youth not yet assigned a role in the world. Luc could barely take his eyes off the child. "Such a sweet young one. So pure and bright. You will do amazing things one day, Micah. I can already tell."

He handed the child back to Ariel, the thump of her relief slamming into his chest. The little pack of three within his pack of fourteen stood as a solid unit once more.

"We are blessed as a pack to have received so much from the fates over the past few years. From our brave Sariel to our giving Charmaine, from our talented Armaita—" Luc shot a grin at Levi's mate "—and yes, I know you prefer Amy."

She nodded, her smoky blond hair falling over her shoulder. "Thank you, Luc."

"And then came Ariel, full of a fierceness of spirit few could exhibit. Michaela, so smart and independent—a true leader among us. And then our lovely and wild Zophiel stole her way into our pack and added her feisty personality to the mix."

"Damn right, I did," Zoe called, leaning against Deus and looking as sassy as ever.

"Yes, you definitely did. Now we have Micah, and the pack feels more complete than ever. We are blessed."

The men of the group all repeated Luc's final line, the love pouring through the room. Luc couldn't have asked for more. His wolf disagreed with that thought, immediately throwing a picture of Cassiel into their shared mind. Something Luc could only ignore as he fought his instincts to focus on his pack.

She is meant to be here. His wolf growled, still trying to overpower Luc's concentration with images of Cassiel.

He could not ignore his pack, though. Which meant he needed to ground himself in them. "Sariel, please tell me how Angelita is doing. We haven't heard much from her lately."

Hours later, after an evening of food and catching up and getting to know one another, Luc sat on the porch with Levi, Phego, and Michaela. Young Levi's mate, Amy, had already gone to bed, her pregnancy tiring her much earlier than normal. Luc had a feeling Levi wanted to talk to him about something. Otherwise, he would have followed his woman to bed like a good mate. Luc could sense the troubled thoughts of the younger Dire Wolf, but he waited for Levi to find his words. To lay out what he needed to feel more confident and surer of his position. It didn't take him long.

"I don't want Amy taking any watch shifts, even if there are others with her." Levi huffed, shaking his head. "She's in a delicate condition."

Michaela's laugh could only be described as boisterous. "She's pregnant, not breakable."

"I know, but…" Levi stared off into the woods, his face growing grave. His expression darkening. "When that nomad shifter took her from me, when I thought she'd been shot…"

Luc rested a hand on Levi's thigh, sensing the distress inside him. Knowing how hard that moment had been, having experienced the rage and panic with the younger shifter. Levi had been protecting Amy when she'd been taken, had been just feet away when a nomad had snuck inside and tried to steal her. That sort of action, that slip, would have unnerved any one of them.

Luc could only reassure his brother. "We would never let her come to harm."

"I know that, but I still want her someplace safe."

Just as had been happening all evening, a picture of Cassiel flashed through Luc's mind. This time, he focused in on her delicate frame and slight build, the kindness of her eyes. He wanted her safe, too. Not that he had the same connection to her that Levi had with Amy, but still…the idea of Cassiel in danger wreaked havoc in his thoughts.

Inside, his wolf whined. They were in agreement, it seemed.

Deus suddenly stepped out of the door, holding it open as he said, "Levi, Amy's cold."

Which was a very polite way to request her mate's presence in her bed. Likely with both of them naked.

Levi jumped to his feet, grinning. "A mate's job is never done."

Phego and Michaela followed him inside, leaving Luc alone with his most trusted packmate. The man who knew most of Luc's secrets. The Dire he'd relied on for years to provide him with whatever he needed—information being the primary focus of those desires.

And he needed information now. "Do you ever remember a mating happening where there wasn't an initial pull to bond? Where one side didn't experience the mating at all?"

Deus sat down beside him, not pushing for more. Not interrogating his Alpha. Simply staring off into the darkness and giving the question serious thought. "There are often matings that aren't acceptable to one or both parties."

"Not that. Not an adversarial partnership. More…like the bond was too quiet to be felt by one party."

"I'm not aware of one, but I could go through the records to see what's been reported over the years." He sat back, supporting his upper body on his straightened arms. "Someone in particular you're thinking about?"

Luc grunted his yes but didn't say more. He didn't need to. Deus would never require such information.

When Deus finally spoke, it was to change the direction of the conversation. "When I was up here with Zoe, you told me to watch my mate. Continuously."

He had because of the pack. The sickness in the air. "The pack is not close."

"How do you know?"

Luc let his senses unfurl a little, teasing Deus with a taste of what he dealt with constantly. "Can you feel that? The sickness around us?"

"Yes."

"That's nothing compared to how strong it was when you were here with Zophiel the first time. I don't sense them as being close to us."

"And the women of their pack?"

The women. Luc's personal slice of hell served up on a frustrating platter. "Still nothing. I can't sense them."

"What if they're not here?"

"They are. I know they are."

"But you can't sense them, and we can't find them." Deus sighed, rising from his more relaxed position. "What are we going to do about the pack?"

Luc worried his lip, letting his instincts spread. Letting his senses dance more on the surface of his mind. Letting the static build into a cacophony only he was subjected to. His distraction sat too deep, though. His mind too caught up in the odd tickling sensation he understood as Cassiel to focus. He had no answers, and that bothered him greatly.

"I need to run."

Deus didn't even blink. "Go. We'll hold down the fort here."

Luc didn't need to be told twice. He shifted on the spot, racing into the shadows as if hell itself were on his heels. The deep darkness of night in the bush soon enveloped him, hiding him from the rest of the nocturnal eyes in the trees. He ran for what felt like hours, jumping over rocks and fallen trees, skidding around turns and splashing through puddles. This was what he needed—what he craved. Freedom. Even if just for a moment. Just enough to clear his head.

He ended up at a spot overlooking the lake from the far end, about in the middle of where his cabin and Cassiel's were situated. He couldn't actually see them—it was far too dark—but he could sense them both. Subtly, a tickle in his brain. Just enough for a taste... And then he truly let his senses go.

Normally, Luc held back his powers—restrained his wolf because his own energy influenced the shifters around him. But this time, he released it. He could feel his packbrothers— one moving closer as if he needed the protection, while the rest gathered at their homestead. Protective SOBs, though he couldn't deny them the desire to keep something so precious to them safe. He also began to feel the bleakness of the pack presence, the darkness within. They seemed closer than he would have thought, but not close enough to be a threat.

More something to pay attention to. And he needed to pay attention—there was no feminine energy coming from the black hole of their presence, but he knew they had two women under their control. Or had. Could they have lied to Deus? No—Luc had sensed them. He'd felt their power and the surety of women in the pack. They had females somewhere; he just couldn't feel them.

Unable to resist the pull to her, he looked out over where Cassiel resided, allowing her presence to dance along his senses. Still weak, but there. His feel of her was tenuous at best. He needed more time in her presence to figure her out, but time was something he didn't have. Especially in the range. This pack—the wrongness within them—had been eating at him for a long time. It could be a danger to his pack, to Cassiel, to everything. He needed to focus.

"You're having trouble with your priorities." Bez morphed from the shadows, the Dire seemingly made of darkness himself. Coming to sit beside his Alpha and look out over the world below.

Luc never had kept much from the shifter. "I am torn in two directions."

"Could she be your mate?"

Deus had either talked—highly unlikely—or Bez had overheard their conversation. He couldn't blame the shifter for being curious—Luc so rarely called all of them together. And though he didn't need to answer the question, he figured he might as well at least attempt to be honest. "I don't know."

"If you're not sure, I have to assume she's not."

And yet...that didn't feel right. "She's something, though. There's a pull to her that I can't explain even though I don't feel the return of it from her. It's...unusual."

"So, figure it out. Then we can all get back to work." Bez rose to his feet once more, placing a hand on Luc's shoulder.

"I want to take my mate home where she's safe. And that's definitely not up here."

"Are any of us safe anywhere, though?"

"So long as I can stand between my mate and what's coming, I have a shot. This pack—the heavy feeling of this range—I don't know where the danger might come from. And neither do you."

Bez walked off into the night, shifting and running back to the homestead. Leaving Luc to sit and think over his words. He didn't know where the danger might come from anymore. He used to—had been positive he could have identified all threats within the pack. Now?

He didn't know anything anymore.

Ten

*D*ays. Luc traveled days through the woods without going back to Cassiel's. Every minute away, every hour without seeing her safe and sound, wore on him even more than the constant pressure of feeling his pack so closely. Of enduring the barrage of their emotions at such close range. Being without Cassiel had quickly become the hardest part of his days.

He didn't stop running, though.

Luc and his pack hunted relentlessly. Chasing shadows through the forest, exploring some of the caves they discovered along the base of the mountains, and investigating every possible paw print and trail leading to the lake. The land spread far, the possibilities for hiding endless, and still, they hunted.

Deus, Phego, and Levi had joined Luc on the morning run, leaving the cabin full of Omegas and their guards behind. The quietness of having his brothers at his side soothed Luc for only a brief moment before the sickness in the forest began to wear on him again. Until it began to eat away at his control. Until he was forced to shift human and sit among the fallen trees to clear his head of everything.

"You okay there, man?" Deus came to sit beside him, the two others standing to the side. Almost surrounding him, as if he were a threat. Someone to worry about. The thought just about made Luc laugh.

"I am tired, brothers. That is all."

He could almost feel the concerned look on Phego's face as he said, "Perhaps we should stop hunting for a few days. Rest and regroup."

But Luc couldn't stop. Couldn't hold off. The woods called to him, Cassiel called to him, his pack called to him. Everything and everyone in a thousand-mile radius called to him. It was all…

"Luc?"

His head throbbed, the sickness around him bearing down harder than ever. The pack was close. He could sense it. Their presence made his brain ache and his body sore, made his wolf almost uncontrollable. Made him want to—

"Is he shifting slowly? What the fuck is going on?"

Luc didn't need to identify the wolf in question—something was wrong with him, and his brothers were seeing it firsthand. Seeing all he'd been trying to hide from them for decades. They would soon know, and then…they'd leave him to die.

He had one last rescue to finish before he welcomed the end. "I need to hunt. I need to find the females."

With that, he shifted again, his wolf taking off at breakneck speed down the ravine. His brothers soon followed, their anxiety persisting into their animal forms. The call of nature, the singing of Mother Earth, embraced Luc as it always had, but the sickness from the pack marred the affection. Gave it a dangerous edge. One that ramped up his senses even more than usual.

He came upon the pack almost by accident. He'd run up another hill and came to a stop with the lake to his right. Below him, moving along the rocky base of one of the cliffs, were twenty wolves. The energy from them hit him hard and without warning, the disease within their pack infecting him. No hope, no future, no way to find the females he still couldn't sense. There was nothing but loss and negative energy, and he could barely breathe through it.

It wasn't until the wolves began howling from below that he realized he'd lost control of his gift. That he noticed he was broadcasting their own chaotic energy back at them. He tried to rein in his power, but it was too late. The damage had been done, and the pack had begun looking for whatever was upsetting them.

The hunters had become the hunted because Luc had lost control.

"Stop," Levi yelled, running up behind him. "Luc, you have to get control of it."

"Fuck me, is this how you feel all the time?" Phego looked horrified, clutching his chest like a man about to keel over from a heart attack. "You can't live like this. No one can live like this."

It was Deus who stepped forward, though. Deus who grabbed him by the scruff of the neck and got right in his face. Deus who cleared the way for his own thoughts and emotions to shine through the mess from the outside.

"Go," he said, his voice strong and almost Alpha order-ish. "Go where your wolf needs to be. Get out of here."

Go. Run. Leave.

So, he did.

The dogs were driving Cassiel crazy.

"What is wrong with you today?" She pushed Moxie—who'd been trying to literally jump into her arms—down for the fifth time. "All of you are acting as if there's a bear on the porch."

Cassiel looked out over the woods, the feeling of unease she'd been suffering from most of the day making her wonder if there could be predators in her woods. She doubted it—the most dangerous ones came out at night, and they wouldn't have hung out all day without attacking. No, this was something else. Something she couldn't see with her own eyes. Something that needed to go away before her dogs drove themselves over the edge with their anxiety.

She was about to head inside for the night when the dogs all began to bark. All began to stand tall and stiff, looking ready to dive into a fight. Definitely something coming. Something not normal. Cassiel raced to the porch to grab the gun she'd left there and spun around, bringing the weapon to her shoulder. Ready to fire if necessary.

Instead of a bear or wolf appearing from the shadows of the forest, though, it was a man. A particular one...one she'd been thinking about a lot. Luc.

Half dressed, filthy, and looking as if he'd run the entire way from his homestead to hers, he stumbled forward. His steps slow and his feet barely rising from the ground. She'd never seen someone look so exhausted in her life.

Cassiel lowered the gun, taking a single step toward him. Raising her voice as she asked, "Are you okay?"

Obviously tormented and unable or unwilling to make sense of words, Luc shook his head. His breaths exploded from his lips, his arms and legs shaking as he tried to move closer. As he took a single step and nearly fell to his knees. That was enough for Cassiel. She set the gun down and raced for him, catching him under the arm and letting him lean his bulk on her as she directed him toward her cabin.

"It's okay. Do you have another migraine? It'll be fine— I'll take care of you. You're here now. It'll all be okay." Or so she hoped.

The few items of clothing Luc wore were torn apart, aged and worn in a jagged sort of way. And wet. In fact, he was shivering from his damp hair and clothes. Good lord, how long had he been outside? And how did he end up half dressed and soaked? It may have been summer in the range, but that still meant the temperature dropped at night. She doubted it was much more than forty degrees outside— comfortable if dressed appropriately, which Luc was not. And he was wet. For all she knew, he could have frostbite.

Cassiel dragged her friend inside the cabin, moving smoothly into survival mode as she laid him on her bed. Cold and wet were a horrible combination, so she did the first thing she knew she needed to.

She stripped the clothes right off Luc's body.

The big man didn't speak, though he grumbled and made sounds like growls as she lifted his legs and tugged the fabric off him. It stuck often enough that she had to touch more of him than he might have liked, had to run her hands over his skin. She tried to keep her thoughts clean, forced herself to remember that something was wrong—he was ill or scared or hunted. He needed help. She tried so very hard to focus on his physical needs instead of her own deepening desires.

"Almost there," she said as she removed the last piece of clothing from his very muscled body.

Luc lay silent on her bed, naked and shaking, as she raced for a thick piece of fur to wrap him in. The warmth it provided would do him good until she could heat up enough water for a bath. *If* she could heat up enough water for a man that size to soak in.

"Here." She tucked another blanket around him and pulled him up to sit on the edge of her bed. "I'll put some water on the fire. Maybe even a sponge bath would help raise your body temperature. I don't know."

But she didn't get the chance to leave him. He grabbed her hand, whispering words in a language she couldn't understand. Sounding so heartbroken and tired and just…not himself. Her skin prickled, awareness of how easily he could overpower her if he chose to making her wary. But this was Luc, and she couldn't see him turning mean. Couldn't see him doing anything to hurt her. So instead of trying to move away, she stepped closer. Ran her fingers into his hair and tugged his head back until she could look him in the eye.

"What happened to you, Luc?"

He shook his head, mumbling something like "too much," before he grabbed her and tugged her down on top of him. She ended up straddling his lap, his head on her chest, his cold body warming under her touch. And she did touch. She let herself be held and held him right back, wrapped her body around his and tightened her grip. Because this was her friend, and he needed her. And deep down, she wanted to be needed.

"Shh," she hushed, running her fingers through his hair. "Warm up with me, then you can talk."

He held her closer, yanking the blanket from between them. Tugging up the bottom of her shirt until their bellies touched, until they were skin-to-skin and she was dying inside. Her hips moved of their own accord, her body reacting to his. But the moment, the embrace, wasn't sexual, so she didn't push things. This wasn't about lust or desire. This was care—intimacy. This was two people coming together to fulfill a need, so she stilled once more. And she held the large man in her arms. And she closed her eyes as she rocked with him and shared her warmth.

And she found a peace in his arms that she'd never once experienced in her life.

Eleven

*L*uc awoke to a feeling he hadn't experienced in a long time, one that soothed his soul and calmed the inner static that had become his constant companion over the years. That feeling was peace.

Cassiel's little cabin sat in utter shadow, completely silent other than the sounds of people and dogs breathing in the night. The stillness of the forest outside assisted in blanketing the world in a hush he had never experienced. His head— usually so loud as the emotions and pulses of the world bored down on him—had little more than a whisper of input dancing inside it. Barely anything, really. Such a change, considering he'd run from his pack mere hours ago because the level had been more like a scream. This wasn't true silence inside his mind—that was something he doubted he would ever find— but it was tolerable. A buzz instead of a chainsaw, a breath instead of a freight train. Totally bearable. What he wouldn't give to live with that level of sound in his head all the time.

Luc's wolf stretched inside his mind, luxuriating in their new reality, no matter how short it might be, both man and beast rested and refreshed. And unable to resist the woman underneath them.

Cassiel must have fallen asleep holding Luc, her legs around his hips and his head on her breasts. Her weight rested on one of his hands, his arm tucked underneath her waist. Her arms wrapped around his shoulders as if to hold him closer. Such a comfortable position for Luc, so intimate for both of them to be touching all over. He liked her holding him this way. Enough to move slightly up her body. To take advantage of their position to sniff. To investigate the woman a little more.

And sniff, he did. He downright nuzzled into her neck, breathing her in. Growling softly under his breath as he immersed himself in the scent of her. Warm and bright, like a flower field on a summer day, her unique smell enveloped him in a sense of connection, a feeling of attraction beyond any he'd ever experienced. But beyond the floral was a scent he knew instinctually. One he'd caught a whiff of before but that was so weak, most of his kind would have missed it.

Wolf. Shifter. Omega.

As his wolf's growl came from deep within his chest, Cassiel moved slightly, a response to him, it seemed. Her next exhale rumbled a tiny bit, just enough to be heard. So much quieter than his, smoother and frail as well, but the telltale language of their kind was there. Weak but not dead.

The pull Luc had been feeling toward Cassiel increased, sending a vibration skittering up his spine. A feeling of need filling his chest. He sniffed again, scenting everything about her. Bringing her essence deep within himself. Focusing hard on the beast within her. The one he could only barely sense. The animal was weak, insipid and feeble, but there. And it was responding to him. It recognized him as one of its own.

Unable to stop himself, Luc shifted lower, bringing his head back down to Cassiel's chest. Letting the vibration of his near-constant growl call to the beast within her. The one who had yet to quiet. There was an underlying strength to the animal—a sense of power that had likely been denied. She'd been starved of life, the little wolf. Locked up inside her human form and neglected or forgotten about. Ignored. That sense of power behind her was strong, though. Much like the inherent strength of the women his brothers had mated with. This girl—this wild woman living in the bush of Alaska—was likely an Omega shewolf.

And even more likely his mate.

The very thought of such a thing floored him. He couldn't have a mate—he'd lived for millennia without one, had traveled the world alone for far longer than he could even remember. But denying his attraction to her was only becoming harder—the fates had tied him to Cassiel, connected them in an unbreakable way. His wolf practically purred for her, even. He would need to figure out how to bring out her own beast, though. How to introduce his woman to his world. Cassiel might not want that, she might—

The woman in question awoke suddenly, her dark eyes finding his immediately. A pulse thumped deep within Luc's gut, a reminder of their connection. A quiet manifestation of their bond as that stare yanked his wolf to the forefront of his mind. Fuck him, they were mated.

"Are you okay?" Cassiel asked, her voice low and soft. A balm over his abused eardrums—one that was most welcome.

Luc couldn't help but notice how she didn't pull away from him. Didn't try to dislodge his body from how it clutched hers to him. He didn't either. "I'm fine. Are you okay?"

"Yeah." She inched down a smidge, bringing her hips to rest under his. Her legs bracketing his thighs. Luc responded on pure instinct, rocking slightly. Teasing her body with his just to see how she'd respond. Her breath caught, her eyes staying locked with his. And she moved with him.

"Cassiel." His whisper sounded like a plea to his own ears, like a needful gasp. And perhaps it had been. The woman in question simply shushed him, bringing a hand to his face to pull him closer. Rolling her hips under his as she tugged him down. As she brushed her soft lips against his. As she made him wait for the taste of her.

"Is this why you came?"

It took Luc a long couple seconds to interpret her words because he hadn't come yet, but he wanted to. Wanted to bury himself inside her heat and make her howl for him. Wanted to slide in deep and see if their bodies were as meant for each other as he assumed they would be.

But that wasn't what she meant. "I came because I needed peace, and I can only ever find it around you."

She stared at him, silent and still. No longer moving. Barely breathing, it seemed. But then she gave in and offered Luc a taste of the heaven he'd never thought he'd experience. "I want to kiss you, Luc."

His mate, the shewolf the fates deemed perfect for him, wanted her lips on his. Wanted to join with him in a small, physical way. His heart practically jumped out of his chest at the thought. "I want to kiss you too, Cassiel."

"So, do it."

"Are you sure?" He rolled forward, his big body more than covering hers. His cock resting just outside of where he wanted it to be. Right up against where he knew he could tease her little body into a mass of nerve endings and pleasure if given the chance. If she consented. "I want to kiss you more than anything, but you may never recover from it."

Cassiel smiled, one side of her lips lifting a little higher than the other. Sarcastic. "You're awfully sure of yourself."

He held her gaze, growing serious. His nose brushing hers. His heart opening in a way it never had before. Mate. His mate. Cassiel was his fated *mate*.

Nothing would ever matter more to him.

"I know I'll never recover from your lips on mine, sweet Cassiel. I'll never stop wanting to taste you once I start."

She tangled her fingers in his long hair, tugging out the strap he used to tie it back and away from his face. Freeing him in some small, yet not insignificant way. "Then perhaps we shouldn't kiss."

"Or maybe we should kiss all the time."

"Maybe we should try it. Just once. See if it's as life-altering as you think."

Luc leaned closer, letting his hips roll into hers, bringing his lips down as slowly as possible. "Are you sure you're ready?"

She stared up at him, looking so small. Not scared, more anxious. Excited, maybe, but with a hint of nerves added in. Just the same way he felt being wrapped in her arms with her lips millimeters away from his. This was the moment—the second that his entire existence was about to shift. He could feel it coming, and he would not do anything to stop it. In fact, he wanted it. More than anything else in the world.

And apparently, so did Cassiel. "Yes."

That word, her consent, was all he needed. He dipped down, stealing her lips. Kissing her softly at first as he learned the touch and taste of her. As he sank into the heaven of the intimate act. The darkness of the wild blanketed them, giving them the illusion of total privacy. Giving Luc the sensation that there was nothing else—just her and him and a kiss that set his soul on fire. With his lips on hers, the world fell completely silent inside his mind. Everything going still so he could focus wholly on Cassiel, on his mate.

Bless the fates for such a gift.

Gripping her, sliding his hands down to clutch her ass, Luc tugged Cassiel even closer. Lined her up more just so he could roll his hips into hers and tease the sweet pussy between her thighs. So he could bump her clit with every pass and bring her pleasure.

She jerked and gasped, her hands shaking as she held on tighter, her kisses growing stronger and deeper with every rock of him against her. Cassiel had quickly become a woman on the brink of losing control, and Luc was determined to push her right over the edge and watch her break all over him.

Their kisses turned deeper, the two locked together in a writhing, humping mass of need. Luc had to pull back to take a breath and to regain control of the growl rumbling within him. Just a quick second to swallow down the sound so as not to scare his woman. Just a moment.

But as Luc fought to regain his control, Cassiel made a move to make him lose it. She dropped her head back, arching her back and exposing her neck to him. The animal side of Luc, the one that saw the pose as a submissive gesture, surged forward, instincts taking over. Luc dove in. Nuzzling her, licking up the column as she grew hotter and wetter against his cock. As she responded to every move of his with arousal and desire. As she pushed all of his buttons—the ones belonging to the man and the ones owned by the beast—without even knowing what she was doing to him. How could he resist such perfection? Why would he want to?

Unable to stop himself, Luc bit Cassiel's neck—softly, a tease instead of a claiming. Cassiel jumped and groaned underneath him, her body going stiff as the new sensation likely flew up her spine. The bite of a human was one thing—the bite of one wolf to another was a totally different experience. He'd heard the stories—knew how mating bites could drive men and women to the heights of ecstasy—and though he wouldn't be breaking Cassiel's smooth, golden skin, he could tease her. He could give her a taste while taking one for himself.

The scent of her wolf grew stronger in the darkness as he

moved his body over hers, as he took in the essence of his mate and shared his with her. The connection between them grew stronger, his heart reaching out for hers. Wanting so badly to make her his in every way he could—physically, spiritually, and sensually. Luc focused on the physical, though—on Cassiel's raspy breaths and the way her hands clutched at him as he kept using his cock against her pussy. On the way she moved with him, her human body responding to his. Her wolf would have to wait—she obviously either didn't know how to shift or didn't want to. He would have to get to the bottom of that, but not yet. Right then, he had one mission. A goal he was already working toward.

He needed to make his woman come.

Twelve

Cassiel knew she shouldn't have started this, shouldn't have initiated intimacy with Luc after he'd shown up at her cabin the way he had. The man had been a literal mess and, had she been a better person, she would have kept her hands to herself. But if touching him was wrong, she would never want to be right.

"Luc," Cassiel whispered as the string inside her—the one running from her clit up her spine to the very top of her head—snapped tighter. Every move of this man, every arch and breath and touch, only made her want more. Made her toes curl and her heart pound. He hadn't even done anything other than dry-hump her, and she was already about to come.

"My sweet Cassiel." Luc made a sound like a growl, something that burned brightly under Cassiel's skin. "Be wild with me. Just this once, be wild."

She wanted to—by the stars, did she want to. And really, there was no reason to deny him. Cassiel nodded, reaching to pull Luc in closer. Mashing her lips to his in a messy, rough kiss as his body continued its assault on hers. He slipped his large, rough hand under her shirt, moving upward slowly. Teasing her with the heat of his touch. And it was hot—so very hot. His entire body burned against hers. She could feel it through her clothes, and she liked it. Enjoyed the way he warmed her.

Wanting more of his touch and his heat and just *him*, she pushed on his shoulders until he sat up a little. As soon as she had space, she reached down and tugged her flannel shirt up and over her head. She had to move her hips to yank it out from under her, seeing as how it was so long, it nearly touched her knees, but Luc gave her the space to do so. Even helping her along the way so she didn't end up tangled in the soft fabric. When she was finished—bare from the waist up—she lay back against the mattress, reaching for Luc once more.

"Cassiel," Luc whispered, staring down at her in what she could only describe as reverence. Running a single finger along her breastbone and making her shiver. "You are so beautiful."

He palmed her, his fingers barely brushing the bottoms of her breasts, his hand flat against her upper stomach. Heat. So much heat. The rough skin of his palm only enticed her more, making her want both sides of him—the soft and the harsh. The gentleman and the wild man. She wanted all of him.

Reaching between them, she slid her hand down his abs, biting her lip at every dip and furrow. The man was muscular, that was for sure. Strong and hard. And long. Her fingertips hit the head of his cock long before she'd expected to, only a thin layer of cotton keeping her skin and his apart. He grunted, looking down, watching what she was doing. Something about that—about his need to see—ramped up her desire. Made her want to give him a show, to tease him until he broke.

Keeping her eyes on him as he kept his on her hand, she

slipped lower still, past the head. Down, down, down until she got to the middle of him, until she had room to grip him fully. Until she could wrap her fingers around his hard cock and press her palm to the thick vein running along the underside.

"Fuck, Cassiel." Luc jerked, practically thrusting into her hand. Releasing a groany sort of rumble as he rocked softly against her. "You're going to make me come if you keep that up."

She squeezed harder. "So?"

Suddenly, Luc grabbed her, pulling her over and rolling until he was underneath her. Until she sat straddling his hips, her hand still palming him.

"So maybe I want to see you come first."

Cassiel gave him one final squeeze before bringing her hands to his shoulders and leaning over to press her lips to his. "Make me."

Never let it be said that Luc couldn't live up to a challenge. With a single tug, he ripped her leggings from her body, releasing another one of those rumbly groans that sounded so much like a growl. Something about that sound spoke to her libido, warming her skin and making her pussy wetter. There was no denying that she liked the rougher side of this man, the animalistic, needy side. No denying it and no need to try. His need heightened hers, making her want to be just as rough and wild. Just as free.

Cassiel sat up straight and rolled her hips, though the feel of his heated flesh against hers brought her up short. "How did you get your underwear off?"

Luc shrugged, grabbing hold of her hips and smiling up at her. His skin pale and his eyes almost silver in the moonlight streaming through the window. "Magic."

Magic, indeed. Laughing, she began her slow rock again. Letting the length of him rub along her most sensitive parts.

Loving the way the head hitting her clit made her entire body tingle. Oh yes, she'd be coming, all right. And soon. There was no denying that.

"Luc," she said as she fell forward, still rocking, her body keyed up and so focused on coming that nothing else mattered. "I want to come. I need to."

"I know, sweet angel. I know." He rocked his hips into hers, undulating his entire body and lifting her on every rise. So much strength. Everything about the man spoke of his power, and she wanted to feel it. Wanted to experience it. Wanted every inch of him to touch every inch of her.

"It's not enough." She shook her head, practically panting with her need to come, frustrated with her inability to.

Luc didn't speak—didn't need to. He grabbed her hips and flipped her again, laying her down in the soft furs she'd put out for his sleeping pallet. Diving down her body and spreading her knees before attacking her pussy with his mouth. And oh god, was it good. So hot and wet and rough just like him. Amazing. He tongued her opening and flicked her clit, bringing her hand into the mix to spread her lips. To slide one thick finger inside her as he continued to lap at her flesh. As he pushed her right along the cliff that would lead to her ultimate pleasure. Her little death at his hands. And mouth.

It didn't take long—maybe a minute, maybe a little more—until she broke, coming hard and wild. Her entire body bowing under the pleasure of it all, garbled sounds that should have been words spilling from her lips as she let loose a throaty groan so very similar to his. He'd made an animal out of her, and she loved it.

"More," she finally said, clutching at his shoulders and trying to pull him up from his place between her thighs. Reaching into the little table beside the bed for the condoms she'd kept there since she'd moved in but never used. "I want more."

Luc took the foil packet without question, ripping it open and sheathing himself before he lifted onto his arms and rocked forward, covering her in his heat. Nudging her entrance. "Are you sure?"

"Yes, yes, yes." She dug her fingers into his muscles, ready to cry from the pleasure, ready to collapse from the desire for another orgasm. "Please, I need you inside me. Please."

"Oh, angel girl. You never have to beg. I'll take care of you." He slid his way inside, staring down at her. Completely focused on her. She couldn't look away either. Couldn't break the intimate moment of their eyes locking together as he slipped inside her. As he stretched and filled her. As they both growled through the connection.

"So thick," she said, writhing a little beneath him as the pleasure began to border on pain in a good way. "How are you so thick?"

Luc chuckled. "It's not me, it's you. You're so fucking tight."

She wrapped her arms around his shoulders and tugged him closer, knocking him off-balance and grunting as the new position put pressure right on her clit. "A matched pair, that's what we are."

Luc groaned and thrust harder, driving himself deeper. "We are. It's exactly what we are."

There was no more time for words, no more room for dirty talk or conversation. There was only them, connected and in motion, both speeding toward their own releases but doing it as a unit. And that race was good—so fucking good. Every inch of Cassiel tingled, every piece of skin burning brightly under the heat of Luc.

Her second orgasm came as a surprise, breaking over her before she was ready to fully accept it. Luc didn't stop, though. He kept thrusting, kept working her over. Moving her legs for a new angle and going harder than before.

"Another," he said as he sat back and rubbed his thumb

over her clit. "Fuck, I love the look of your pleasure. Give me another."

And so it went—she would come, grabbing for his flesh and sometimes yelling his name, and he'd move, throwing her body into another shape. Forcing them into another position and going back to fucking her hard and fast. He had more stamina than any man she'd ever even heard of, more strength than any she'd seen. And he had all of that power and endurance focused one hundred percent on her.

It was glorious.

And exhausting.

"Luc, please." She writhed beneath him, her hip muscles sore and her pussy starting to ache. "I want you to come."

"Are you surrendering, angel?" He leaned down to give her a deep, wet kiss before pulling away with a growl. "I've wanted to come for so long now. Are you sure? Have I satisfied you enough?"

Oh hell, those words made her tingle. "Yes. I'm sure. Come for me."

Luc groaned and grabbed her leg, bringing her foot to his shoulder and kissing along her ankle. "One more, then I'll come. Give me just one more."

She didn't think she could. Didn't know if her body had any more to give, but she nodded anyway. Grabbed hold of his arms and moved her body with hers to try to climb that hill one more time. She rocked and hissed and chanted his name as he groaned louder and louder and fiercer. It was when that rumble turned to some sort of snarl that she finally broke again, something deep inside her waking up to the sound and howling in response. The two of them came together, both making noises that didn't sound human, both shaking and holding on to the other. Cassiel had never felt anything like that last orgasm—had never allowed herself to be so free and wild with someone else. But she had let loose with Luc, and that freedom—that full-out release—had felt amazing.

Afterward—after a quick cleanup and a move to her little bed where they practically had to lie on top of each other for them to fit—Cassiel stayed awake and stared down at the man who'd somehow stolen her heart already. Where had he come from? How had he gotten her to trust him so quickly? She didn't know, but what she did know was that her heart had been stolen—taken by the man asleep on her chest.

She ran her hands through his shaggy hair, smiling. Unable not to enjoy the quietness of a sleeping Luc in her arms. This was it—her soul mate. The man she was meant to be with. She knew it—could feel a connection to him unlike any other she'd ever known. The very thought terrified her, but she knew then and there that there would be no stopping it. Luc was going to change her life, drag her soul back to the holy wild and release something inside her that she hadn't known was there. He was going to upset her orderly little world.

And she couldn't wait for him to start.

Thirteen

The dogs seemed very excited to see Luc up and about in the morning, or else he was simply projecting his good mood onto them.

"You're such a good girl." Luc rubbed Moxie's ears the way she liked as the dog rested her front paws against his stomach. The poor thing was so little compared to the others and yet the one most filled with love for the people around her. "Was she the runt of the litter?"

Cassiel moved closer, her body brushing his. Seemingly unable not to touch. "No, but the pups in her litter were all sort of small. Don't doubt her, though—she's fast and strong and will run for days on end. I'd take ten of her over most of my other dogs."

"Really?"

"Yeah." Her face grew serious, and she scrunched up her nose. "I mean, I'd still keep my other dogs."

Luc laughed. "Of course you would." He gave Moxie one more good rub then guided her down, moving through the outdoor pen with Cassiel at his side. "What else needs to be done?"

She looked over the little homestead, still bumping into him, making him the happiest man on the planet knowing she wanted to be close. "I need to chop up some of the dried fish for their breakfast."

He linked his fingers with hers, tugging her closer. "Show me how I can help."

Cassiel led him to her drying racks, where rows upon rows of dried Arctic char and salmon hung above their heads. She reached for a ladder leaning against a support post, but Luc pulled her to a stop.

"I can get them for you. Just show me which ones."

They worked together for a while—him pulling down the selected fish and bringing them to Cassiel and her chopping them into manageable chunks with a wicked looking cleaver. The morning was cold but not uncomfortably so, and Luc enjoyed working out in the fresh air. He even liked getting slobbered on by the dogs. He especially liked watching his mate live her everyday life.

His mate. By the fates, how had that happened?

"So tell me," Cassiel started, knife still in hand and fish pinned down on the table. "What happened last night that ended with you running to my place half dressed?"

He was still half dressed—still needing to get back to his homestead so he could pull himself back into his costume of a wilderness man. Of a human. So he could lie to her a little better.

He hated this part.

"I was tracking something in the woods when I realized I had somehow become the one being tracked."

"You see what it was?"

"Nope. Just heard the rustling. I tried to make a lot of noise to scare it, but that didn't work, so I started moving away. Then I started running." Luc thought about what had really happened—the pack, his Dires, the noise he couldn't escape from. The pressure that had nearly broken him and how he'd thrown all that emotion out into the world, riling the others up. How he'd run to try to escape the input. Run straight to Cassiel's front door. "I'm not sure why I ended up here, but I'm glad I did."

"I'm glad you did too." She stretched up onto the balls of her feet, obviously angling for a kiss. Luc would never be one to deny her. He crouched lower, taking her mouth. Tasting her and pulling her soft body against his. He wanted them both naked again, wanted to pin her underneath him and have his way with her or let her climb on him and ride until she broke. He *wanted*. He couldn't get enough of her, couldn't stop the burning of desire in his gut for her.

But eventually, she ended the kiss and pulled away. Giving him a smile. One that captivated him, made him lose all sense of time and place. Had they been the only two people in the world, he wouldn't have been surprised or disappointed.

Cassiel had work to do, though. "Come on, mountain man. Let's finish feeding the dogs."

He snuck in for one last kiss before patting her ass. "Lead the way, mountain woman."

But as Cassiel doled out fish and some sort of soupy water to her sled dogs, Luc began to wonder about her. To want to know her better. To need information.

"Where did you grow up?"

Cassiel turned and raised an eyebrow. "In Alaska."

Defensive. Huh. "I want to know you better, Cassiel. Where in Alaska?"

She sighed and moved on, her face growing darker. Her expression flattening. "All over. I was a foster kid, and I got bounced around. A lot."

A wolf shifter in foster care. Wolves tended to live in packs. If a young pack pup had somehow ended up without parents, the rest of the pack would normally step up to raise the child. Her being alone and in the state system was extraordinarily unusual.

"What happened to your parents?"

"No clue. I was placed in the system before my second birthday and stayed there—no one ever came to claim me, and no family was ever found."

Abandoned so young. It hurt Luc's heart to even think about. "That had to be hard."

She shrugged, as if trying to play off what growing up without a place or a pack had done to her, but Luc knew. He knew a lot more than she did because he understood both human and wolf group dynamics. Cassiel had been starved of her pack at both ends of her intertwined spirits.

"There were good houses, and there were bad ones." She pushed a large dog to the side when he got a little too excited for his breakfast before dropping the fish into his bowl. "But most of them were in the woods, so at least I had that."

"Is that why you're afraid of wolves? Because of being in the woods so much?"

Cassiel laughed and shook her head. "No. The wolves in the woods never bothered me. It was the one in the house that made me fear them."

In the house... "What do you mean?"

"I know it seems crazy—and trust me, my foster family made sure to let me know how crazy it made me sound—but one of my earliest memories is of being alone in my room in the middle of the night and watching a huge gray wolf walk in the door."

Luc's blood ran cold, his brain picking up speed. "The animal just walked in. As if it lived in the house."

"Yup—exactly. Like it was totally normal for a wild animal to be inside."

"What did it do?"

She frowned, turning her head to catch his eyes. "What do you mean?"

"I mean after it walked in…what did it do? Did it sniff you and lick you or—"

"I actually don't remember that." She pursed her lips, looking off into the distance as if trying to recall. "My only memory is the animal walking into the room—taking up the whole darn doorway, to be honest—and then turning to leave."

Which would have meant the wolf in her room had to have been a shifter. Perhaps the local pack had caught her scent and come to investigate, or maybe it had been someone from the pack she'd been born into, checking on her. Whatever the reason, that wolf appearing in her room started to line up the pieces of Cassiel's past in Luc's head.

"That had to be terrifying for you."

Cassiel shrugged again—a defense mechanism, for sure—as she led Luc back to where she stored all her supplies for feeding the dogs. "It was, and I grew up not wanting anything to do with the animals because of it."

"But you like dogs."

"No, I love dogs. Especially mine."

At a loud yip, Cassiel hurried off toward the pen, helping the dog who'd gotten a little tangled in the chains she used when she fed them. Luc, meanwhile, hung back, thinking about his mate. Worrying about her inner wolf. He could call the beast forward and force a shift on her—he was an Alpha after all—but Cassiel would likely be terrified of the change. She would probably fight it, and that could lead to some horrifically slow shifts, causing far too much pain. Not what he wanted her to experience.

Besides, taking away Cassiel's choices wasn't anything he intended to do. He would need to tease out her wolf, allow the beast the chance to grow a little stronger. Give Cassiel the opportunity to realize she was more than human over time. Luc still dreaded the conversation he knew would have to happen—the one where he explained what they were and how her greatest fear lived inside her. And that another of the creatures wanted her by his side forever.

"So," Cassiel said as she sauntered back over to him, looking so damn happy and joyful. "How long can you stay?"

Luc tugged her against him, nuzzling into her neck. Growling softly enough so her wolf could hear him. And she definitely heard him—Cassiel's entire body went hot, her scent deepening. This was his mate, his fated match, and he was going to do anything it took to make her aware and comfortable of the world she would end up being a part of. But slowly and carefully. No way could he rush this.

So he gave her a kiss on the neck, and he held her tight for a few moments. And he stopped growling so her wolf could resettle. The silence brought with it a sense of unease, though. A definite feeling of something wrong in the area. In the woods. His heightened senses picked up a disturbance far closer than any should have been, which meant he needed to shift and figure out what was going on.

He needed to leave Cassiel.

This was going to be harder than he'd ever have expected. "I should really get back soon. I need to figure out what that was in the woods."

Cassiel could hardly look at him, her heartbreak clear. "Right. Yeah, okay. I can just—"

Luc grabbed her and kissed her again, deeply this time. Making his claim clear before pulling away. "I will be back, Cassiel. I need to deal with a few things at camp, then I'll be back. I promise."

Her sad expression faded a little. "Sure. Of course. You have biology research to do."

A giant ball of guilt for the lies he'd told her lodged itself in his throat, so he nodded his agreement. Giving himself an extra moment to swallow it down. "Next time, we'll finish our conversation, and I'll tell you all about my childhood—sound fair?"

Cassiel finally smiled at him, the sorrow leaving her pretty face. "Yeah. It does. Have any idea of when you'll be back? I can pull out some extra meat for a stew and make some bread."

He pulled her in again, his hands on her ass. "You tempt me, woman."

"I try."

"You succeed." One more kiss, one more soft growl, and then he let her go. "Tomorrow. I'll be back tomorrow, okay?"

She wove her fingers together as he backed away, looking smaller than ever in that moment. "Tomorrow is great."

It wasn't—it was too long. He didn't want to leave her at all, but he needed to get back to his camp to talk to his pack, figure out what was wrong in the woods, and get the necessary supplies together to keep Cassiel thinking he was a human. Not at all a light day's work but one he needed to dive straight into, which was why he didn't linger. He kissed his mate one last time then headed for the woods.

"Hey, Cassiel?" he hollered before he hit the tree line.

She turned, cocking her head. "Yeah?"

"Maybe tomorrow you can take me out on that sled of yours."

"The dogs would like that."

"And you?"

She grinned. "I like doing anything with you."

Luc couldn't hold back his own smile, so he blew her a kiss before turning and running into the woods. He had found his mate. So many years alone, but he'd found her. The bond was weak, as was her wolf, but he'd feed it. He'd take such good care of it. And someday, he'd tell Cassiel about his wolf and hers, then he'd do his best to make her feel safe enough to shift. He'd take care of her through every second.

But first, he needed to deal with whatever was wrong in the forest.

He shifted once he was far enough away to feel safe doing so, racing along the path toward Bettles, and immediately felt the local pack. The sickness. The danger they posed. He raced toward his homestead, letting his senses reach out. Feeling for the boundaries. They were close, that pack. Too close. And moving toward him instead of away. He sensed no feminine energy still, but that wasn't his top priority at the moment. The pack had made a move on the Dires' homestead—had come close enough to be a threat. His brothers, their mates, the baby—all could have been in danger. All were under threat. And Luc wasn't there to protect them.

The lead ball in his gut grew ten times larger.

Luc's wolf snarled viciously and pumped his legs harder, the rage at the very idea of a pack threatening his own fueling his speed. He could sense his Dires—feel them running toward him. The entire pack, it seemed. Out in the woods and vulnerable to attack.

No fucking way. No one put his brothers and family in danger. No one got that close to them and lived to tell the tale.

If the pack had identified his home and come looking for a fight, they'd get one. And they'd lose.

Fourteen

*I*t didn't take long—maybe an hour at most—for Cassiel to truly miss having Luc around. Odd considering how long she'd been alone in the bush. But she couldn't deny the longing inside her to see him, to feel him close. One night with him in her bed, and she couldn't imagine spending another one alone.

She tried to ignore the feeling—tried to keep busy and pretend everything was fine—but eventually, the yearning grew too strong to ignore. She wasn't a woman who sat around waiting for anything. She worked for what she wanted, and if that meant hooking up her dogs to her sled and taking a ride around the lake to make sure he'd made it home okay, that was what she would do. Even if it did possibly label her as clingy.

"I just want to make sure he's safe," Cassiel said to Moxie as she clipped her harness into place. "These woods are dangerous. He ran here after being chased by something— he needs to be more careful."

Because he hadn't been armed. Because he hadn't even been dressed appropriately. Because he'd somehow made it to her cabin through the woods and the cold and the wild with some sort of predator chasing him.

Nothing about last night's story fit, and yet she wasn't as worried about that as she was about making sure it didn't happen again. She'd figure out Luc's truth later; right then, she just wanted to find him.

"Ready, team?" Her dogs yipped and jumped, all seeming excited to go for a run. This was what they had been bred for after all. This was their love. "Hike!"

The trip started off well enough—the dogs were excited and energetic, so she spent much of the ride simply trying to keep them all moving in the right direction and working as a team. But as they raced deeper through the woods, as they had to begin to cut a path through the ankle-deep snow that never seemed to melt, she noticed a problem. The dogs seemed anxious, nervous even. At first, she thought her lead dog was choosing not to lead, but that didn't seem accurate. It wasn't the lead dog at all. Bert, her usual swing dog—the one in the second spot—kept wanting to stop. Being that Bert was one of her more sensitive dogs, that shouldn't have surprised her, but it did. They'd run through these woods a thousand times, had raced past scenes far more nerve-racking than the current one. This was not a normal ride.

Fearing Bert might end up pulling the entire sled off track, Cassiel stopped the ride and stepped off the runners.

"Let's try to realign things, shall we?" She unhooked Bert from his spot in swing and moved him to the back, giving him Moxie's spot and bringing her to the front. She was just clipping the smaller dog's harness to the ganglines when she saw them. Prints. Large paw prints. Lots of them. They followed along the trail, some larger than others. Some almost dwarfing her own dogs. She knew the shape of those prints—knew how big the animal had to be that made them.

"Wolves." She hurriedly got Moxie into position and ran back to her sled. She needed to find Luc and get them out of there. A pack of wolves—of large wolves—could take them all down, her dogs included. Thankfully, she'd brought her rifle with her. When she got to the sled, she made sure it was fully loaded and moved it to a more convenient spot. Her dogs seemed even more anxious sitting still the way they were, so she mushed them on. Racing down the trail and hoping against hope she could catch up with Luc before the wolves did.

The dogs ran better with Moxie in swing, all of them working together to fly down the trail. The sled rocked a bit at times, but Cassiel couldn't slow down. She was risking tipping over, but that wouldn't stop her. Luc was out there—alone and in danger. Something inside her told her she needed to hurry, to get to him. To protect him. A ridiculous idea seeing as how he was so much bigger and stronger than she was, but she had her rifle and the knowledge of living in the bush for so many years. She could be of help to him for sure.

The trail dipped down into a shadowy patch of woods before rising once more on a slow incline. The dogs kept running, kept a solid pace both down and uphill, but as they slid over the crest, Cassiel pulled them to a stop, and her heart started pounding.

Wolves.

Lots of them.

Too many for her to deal with alone, but she didn't really have a choice.

Without taking her eyes off the pack of predators, Cassiel reached and picked up her gun. Bringing it to her shoulder and eyeing down the barrel. Her dogs danced in their lines, whining and growling. Understanding the danger they were facing but not running away. She had a solid team that would wait for her instructions to a point, but eventually, instinct would take over. She knew that, understood the whys of it, too. She only had a few minutes to clear the trail or things would be taking a turn for the very, very bad.

With one hand, she slowly, carefully, reached down to grab her ganglines in case her dogs bolted. Keeping her gun sighted on the wolves before her. My god, were they huge. Way too tall and thick for your average Alaskan wolves. They incited an instinctual fear within her, reminding her of being that tiny child and seeing that massive wolf come strolling in as if it had owned the house. As if it had been normal for a beast to be inside.

She would not allow these to get that close.

"You'd better take off, or I'm going to shoot." She had no idea why she spoke—it wasn't as if the creatures understood the English language—but she felt the need to give them a chance to leave. To run off. They didn't, though there was a shift in their positioning. Some of the wolves—the largest ones—stepped in front of others. As if protecting the smaller creatures. No way could she be reading that correctly—they were mindless beasts. And yet…

One wolf in particular, a massive dark animal with eyes darker than the night sky, stared right at her. Refusing to back down. She stared back, knowing this was a power move. Understanding that wolf was probably the leader. The Alpha.

If she took him down, the rest would likely scatter.

She aimed her gun and brought her head down to sight properly before disengaging the safety. One shot was all she'd need, more than likely. One kill, all that had to happen to save herself, her dogs, and likely Luc. If they hadn't already taken him down. A thought that had her finger itching on the trigger.

But then something changed. The wolf never broke his

stare, but he…changed. Switched forms right before her eyes. He went from a giant, furry beast on four legs to a man. To skin and muscle and bone.

To Luc.

A very tall, strong, and naked Luc.

"You…" She shook her head, gun still raised, hands shaking. "You're…"

But words wouldn't come. They couldn't form through the confusion in her mind. This couldn't be happening. It wasn't possible. Luc was a man, not an animal. And yet, she'd just seen him change from wolf to human, had witnessed it herself. No one else was telling her she hadn't seen what had just happened—it was only her. Her mind refusing to make sense of the situation.

Luc had been a wolf and then had shifted human. This was the stuff of horror movies.

The man in question took a single step forward, reaching out a hand in her direction. "It's okay, Cassiel."

"This is so far from okay." She adjusted the gun on her shoulder, still not dropping it. Still aiming. "What the hell is going on here?"

The wolves behind Luc followed him as he inched closer. She couldn't figure out where to focus—on Luc, on the beasts behind him, on her own dogs who seemed ready to run at any second. There was just too much to take in.

"You can put that down," Luc said, his voice soft and soothing. Disturbingly so. "They won't hurt you or your dogs."

As if she could trust him now. "Lies."

A wolf behind him growled, setting the dogs to barking and making them jump. Cassiel held the ganglines tight, stumbling slightly. Luc turned and snarled, a vicious rumble bubbling up from deep with him. The sound something from her nightmares. There was no thought to her actions, no plan or intent. Her legs shook, her weight shifted into her heels, and her finger squeezed the trigger.

Luc stumbled back, blood erupting from his chest. Nightmare intensified. Cassiel grabbed the ganglines tighter as her team all jumped in unison, almost missing the fact that most of the other wolves in the pack facing her shifted to their human forms. Eight naked humans stood before her, all rushing toward Luc, who had slumped to the ground before falling forward. The snow around him turning an angry shade of red. Two of the humans—two women— rushed her sled. Before she could fire off another shot, before she could even tear her eyes away from the heartrending sight of Luc facedown in the snow—they grabbed her and yanked her off her sled.

"Why did you fire?" one of them said, a growl in her voice. She looked…pretty. Gorgeous, even, with long blond hair and a face one might see in a magazine. She also seemed mad as hell. "Why would you shoot at him?"

"We need to move," another woman said, this one dark and equally as gorgeous but in a different sort of way. She appeared stronger, more in control. More demanding. "Phego and Bez, get Luc on the sled. We'll mush him back to the cabin."

That made Cassiel's heart drop. "You're not taking my dogs."

A man—hugely tall and thick and with an air of absolute magic practically oozing off him—stared right at her. His silver eyes making her shiver. "We will take what we need to care for Luc, which includes you. Now, get ready. We'll run alongside."

They dropped Luc into her sled, his bloody chest rising and falling, though slowly. Shallowly. The dark woman crawled in with him, frowning. Holding her hands over the wound and pushing down.

"Go," she yelled. Cassiel reacted on instinct, cueing the

dogs to run even as the rest of the humans all shifted to their wolf forms. Racing through the woods with one beast in the lead of them all.

Running with the wolves who seemed to be trying to save Luc's life.

Fifteen

If Luc had learned one thing on his trek through Alaska, it was this—Phego's mate was not a woman to be trifled with, especially when she lost her temper. As she had when Luc refused her advice.

"You're going to feel that ball of metal in your lung every day for the rest of your life if you don't let me operate to remove it." Dr. Michaela was definitely in the house. She and Ariel were both glaring Luc's way, as if his refusal was a personal attack on their skills. But Luc didn't doubt they could pull him through and have him up and running as quickly as possible. He simply wasn't prepared to be knocked out in any way. Not with Cassiel there. Not with a pack of sick shifters on the move toward them.

No, he wasn't about to let them put any drugs in him. "Not today, Michaela."

At his voice, a whimper sounded from across the room, and both women turned along with him to look. Cassiel sat on a chair in a ball of human flesh, shaking and looking almost ready to cry. Luc wanted nothing more than to run to her, to soothe her fears. To remind her of who he was and how much he cared about her.

But his senses wouldn't allow him to weaken even for a moment. The pack had moved closer and was still heading directly toward them. As much as he cared for Cassiel and wanted her safe, as much as he knew his mate needed protection, she couldn't be his only concern. He had a houseful of people to worry about... starting with baby Micah and a pregnant Amy.

There was a lot to do to keep his pack safe.

"Michaela," he whispered, trying hard not to let the other wolves in the house hear him. "Get the baby, Ariel, and Amy upstairs. Keep them up there. Take care of them."

Michaela eyed him hard, never letting him escape her knowing gaze. "And your mate?"

Because of course she'd figured out what he had yet to tell them all. "Take Cassiel also. I don't think she can shift, and her wolf is definitely weak."

The doctor huffed. "I could have told you that with one look at her. That poor baby wolf has been starved for a lot of years."

Luc sometimes forgot how much knowledge was held by the collective of his pack. He never doubted them; he simply assumed he knew more because he'd been alive the longest. He was willing to admit that he could be an idiot at times.

"Can that be changed?" he asked, leaning in to attempt privacy. "If she learns to accept her wolf, can the animal be strengthened?"

Michaela glanced in Cassiel's direction before shooting him a concerned look. "I've seen it done, but accepting is hard for people who were brought up in the human world and never had contact with their inner beast. You're going to have to be really patient with her."

Luc nodded, knowing patience wasn't his strongest trait but willing to do anything. His mate deserved his best.

Michaela sighed and threw away the gloves she'd been wearing as she'd examined him. Not looking directly at him. Lowering her voice even more. "They're coming, aren't they?"

The pack. The bad one. The threat. Luc nodded.

She shook her head, chancing a look in Phego's direction. "Your brothers are going to be pissed about this. Especially Thaus and Levi."

Because he'd allowed the women to make the decision whether to come or not, and now they were in danger. "I know."

Michaela held out a hand, helping to pull him to his feet and making sure he was steady before collecting the baby, Ariel, and Amy to head upstairs. Every male in the room stiffened when the little troop mounted the stairs, every wolf recognizing what Luc had asked Michaela to do. Waiting for Luc to tell them what the hell was going on.

But his pack would have to wait for another minute before he addressed them—Luc had a mate to care for. Even if just for a moment.

He approached the little human slowly, carefully, keeping his steps light. She didn't cower or shrink back, which Luc took as a good sign. Once he reached her, he dropped to his knees so he could look her in the eye.

Cassiel took control of the conversation. "You're not a biologist."

"No."

"Is your name even Luc?"

"It's what my friends call me," he said, knowing how bad this all looked. "My real name is Lucifer."

Cassiel blinked, her head rising a little. "Like the devil."

"Like the demon—the fallen angel—yes. Though, I've carried many names over the years as languages have died and been reborn."

"You're immortal?"

"No. Not how humans believe. We simply live a very long time."

"How long?"

"Hard to say. I'm not even sure exactly what year I was born."

"But it was a long time ago?"

He shrugged, time being such a relative thing. "Handfuls of centuries, I guess."

Her huff of laughter carried a tone of sarcasm that was undeniable. "Why did you lie?"

Luc inched closer, softening his voice. "Do you really have to ask that?"

Because he'd seen her hate and fear of the animal he carried within him. He'd heard how much she hated those predators in her woods. How she didn't trust them. Why did he lie? How could he not?

Cassiel sat and stared for a long time, looking for something Luc had no way to give her. At least not until she said, "You're a wolf."

Not a question. A statement. A demand of his agreement.

Luc nodded once. "Yes, but only sometimes."

Cassiel huffed, angry, pulling her arms tighter around herself as if in protection. "I want to go home now."

This would not go well. "You can't."

She stabbed him with a look filled with fire, with anger. With fight. "Why the hell not?"

"Because there are more wolves, shifters like me, in the forest. It's why I came up here. They're here, they're coming this way, and they're dangerous."

"So? You're dangerous."

"Not to you, I'm not."

That softened her a little, though she didn't seem the least bit happy. Something Luc had a feeling he'd be paying penance on for a long damn time.

"What about my dogs?"

"Taken care of." Thaus—bad attitude and all—stormed in at that moment, looking positively livid but bringing the sled dogs with him. "Bez said to bring these little ones inside."

Luc sat back, letting the dogs swarm Cassiel. Letting her reunite with her team. Her family. "Thank you, Thaus."

But the shifter didn't turn and walk away. He stared hard at Luc, his lip curling in a sneer as he asked, "Is this it? Are they coming here?"

There was no way for Luc to deny that fact. "Yes."

"Ariel is here. My son." Thaus clenched his hands into fists, looking ready to tear the roof off the house. "You invited Ariel here with our child."

There was no way for Luc to argue that. "I know."

Thaus took a deep breath, the rage inside him a physical force banging its way inside Luc's head. All his brothers seemed to be experiencing stronger emotions than usual, which shouldn't have surprised Luc. Every one of them was worried.

Thaus especially, it seemed. "I'll deal with you later. After the fight." He turned and stormed out of the house, heading back out into the night with Levi on his heels.

"Your friends are mad at you," Cassiel said as she sat with Moxie in her lap.

What Luc wouldn't give for one stroke of that hand on his skin. Alas, he had not earned that back yet. "They are. They're afraid for their mates."

"I'm afraid for my dogs."

"I know. But they're inside and safe." And he would do anything to keep it that way. "You can take them upstairs with you."

"You're sending me upstairs?"

"Wolves are coming. Bad ones." He reached for her,

checking his motions when she flinched back. "I just want to keep you safe."

The woman seemed pissed, seemed so angry with him, but she still leaned forward. Still gave him a tiny kiss on the lips. One that made his wolf howl and his skin go molten.

But then she spoke. "I am so mad at you."

"You have a right to be." Luc stole one more kiss before rising to his feet. "Go. Stay up there. I promise to talk more after I deal with what's coming."

But Cassiel was not a woman to be told what to do. "What if I don't want you to talk to me? What if I leave as soon as this fight is over instead?"

Stunned, heartbroken, his wolf howling inside him, Luc said the only words he could think of. "I would honor your wishes, of course. Even if the very thought of losing a single minute with you makes my heart want to die right here in my chest."

Cassiel didn't respond. She simply stared at him for a long moment, then headed for the stairs with her six dogs trailing behind her. Leaving Luc with his pack. Well, most of them.

"Sariel, Charmaine, and Zoe—why don't you go on upstairs with the others?" Luc took a good look around the room, becoming more anxious as the feel of the pack approaching grew stronger. "This cabin will be our stronghold. No one will pass us to gain access."

Zoe never had been one to hold her tongue. "Apparently you've never watched horror movies."

Sariel chuckled. "Thankfully, none of us is the type to go running slowly through the woods while falling down every twenty feet. We'll fight back if someone gets in here."

All three of the women followed Luc's direction, heading upstairs while chatting as if this were any other night. As if they weren't about to fall under attack by a rogue pack. As if Luc's own mate—trapped in human form and afraid—wasn't up there and unable to fight off a wolf shifter.

If any one of them got hurt, Luc would never forgive himself.

And if the one hurt was anyone other than his own mate, his pack would never forgive him either.

With his heart heavy and his mind cluttered, Luc headed outside to join the rest of the Dires. None looked happy to see him, Thaus and Levi throwing some serious glares his way. They were his brothers—his team—and they would all fight together, whether they were happy about it or not.

But first, Luc had words to say. "Your women are strong and vibrant, filled with the power of the Omega and such gifts to our pack. I am sorry if my actions have put them in danger, and I will do everything I can to make sure they walk away from this fight as whole as they are now." He looked up, making eye contact with each wolf in turn. "I will lay down my own life for any one of them. You have my word."

The feeling outside calmed, the wolves all accepting Luc's words. Which was good, because he'd meant them. If anyone was to die in the fight, it would be him.

Bez finally broke the silence. "Fine. Except no one is fucking dying tonight unless they're from this other pack."

"Right," Levi said with a nod. "No dying. It should be a rule or something."

Thaus still seemed angrier than the others, more worried as well. He had solid reasons to be—two of them. A mate and a child. So it wasn't a surprise when he said, "We figure about a mile out. You sure you're ready for this?"

Luc let his mind wander, let his senses unfurl. Allowed himself to focus on the people upstairs in the house. About pregnant Amy, bringing another blessing to their pack. About Sariel with her sweet smile and freckles; Charmaine and her beauty and huge heart. About Ariel, her bravery in the face of all that fear, and her precious angel baby Micah, who had yet to come into his masculine energy. Michaela and her fierceness. Zoe and her wit. Cassiel, his mate. His one true match who had a backbone of iron. He let his senses connect to all of them, including his brothers. Bringing his entire family into himself and letting their energy fuel his.

He could not let them down.

"I'm ready."

Sixteen

*L*uc stood with his Dire brothers, overlooking a small valley of sorts halfway between their homestead and the oncoming threat. They'd chosen the higher spot as a tactical advantage, a natural impediment to the other pack's progress. No Brooks Range wolf was getting up their hill, because if they did, they had a pretty easy run to the cabin where the women were. It simply wasn't happening.

Without fear of the resulting chaos or personal consequences, Luc pushed his senses a little further, a little harder. He ratcheted his so-called gift to a higher level so he could get a bead on each and every wolf in the pack approaching them. Had he been asked, he would have denied searching out feminine energy, but it would have been at worst a lie and at best an exaggeration. He wasn't intentionally looking for the women, but he certainly took the time to verify the gender presentation of the energy of the pack. No females. Only males. Angry ones. Scared ones. Good—they should have been scared. The Dires were pumped, pissed off at the threat the pack had enacted against them, and ready for war.

"Lungs okay?" Bez asked, not looking at Luc. Keeping his gaze trained on the tree line across the valley.

"Lungs okay." Not a lie—his lungs felt fine. His rib cage and the muscles in his chest, on the other hand, ached like a motherfucker. Being shot in the chest certainly wouldn't kill a shifter, but it hurt. It hurt a lot. As did the very thought of Cassiel leaving to go home without him.

Not something he could worry about right then.

"They're here." His warning came out as barely more than a whisper, but his team tensed. Their determination and rage palpable. Every one of them locked on the far tree line, waiting for the first sign of an attack.

There was no attack, though. A few scraggly wolves crested the hill opposite the Dires and stopped, staring at the pack assembled. Then a few more. And a handful more. There was no denying the pack was hungry—their mangy coats and visible ribs and hips proved that—but they were also sick with some sort of illness that seemed to affect them all the way down to their souls. They were weak and easy to control, yet they still threw Luc's energy into a state of chaos he could barely handle. His power could soothe or inflame the beasts around him, which meant he had a fine line to walk for this meeting. The last thing he wanted was to broadcast that sense of sickness out into the world.

Thankfully, Bez always knew when to run the show for him. "Brooks Range pack. What are you here for?"

One wolf, a man Luc didn't recognize, shifted human, his scraggly wolf changing slowly—painfully—into an even more scraggly human. Thin. The man was far too thin. "You are stalking our woods and hunting in our territory. Your packmate has already killed two of ours. We're here to ask you to leave."

Luc didn't speak, knowing the packmate he mentioned had been Deus, who stood toward the end of their line. The Dire was filled with a rage that took Luc a second to understand, but then he remembered. His Zoe had run into this pack, a man named Rudkin, in particular. The one who'd told Deus about the two females, who'd tried to add Zoe to that number. Who should have been dead for dropping such a threat on a mated female shifter. Deus held strong, though—not attacking or rushing their line. No way would Deus let the man escape a second time, but no Dires had yet to make a move. They could be patient. No need to fuel the pack's fire just yet.

Bez stood tall and strong, arms crossed over his chest and his voice sure as he called out, "We're here on NALB business."

The thin man shook his head. "We're not part of the NALB and cede no jurisdiction."

But it was another male, another rough-looking specimen that had shifted from his wolf state to human and had some sort of tic or twitch in his arm, who fucked up. "The NALB isn't law up here, and we made that clear to your packmate last time we saw him. We also put our claim on any women in our territory." The mood shifted, Twitchy taking a step closer—just one—and taking a big, deep breath. "You brought females with you."

The thunderous rumble of Luc's pack growling in response filled the night air and quieted every other creature in the valley. All seven males leaned forward a little, ready to fight. Ready to kill anyone who threatened their mates. And for the first time, Luc was included in that number—he had a mate back at the cabin too, and no fucking way were these animals getting anywhere near her.

Deus took the lead on the Dires' response, though. "You will not come near our mates, Rudkin. You or your pack. If you try, we'll bury you."

Luc eyed the walking dead man head to toe, sizing him up. Knowing Deus would be taking on that fight. He'd win, too. There was no doubt in Luc's mind.

The thin man glared at Rudkin, raising his hands, palms out, as if trying to block the Dires. "We do not threaten your women. We ask you to leave. Your presence upsets our pack."

But Luc had reached the end of his patience. His senses were still swirling deep into the forest, the sickness this pack carried stirring something dark and painful inside him. The lack of feminine energy driving him absolutely mad.

He couldn't hold his tongue. "Where are the women?"

The Brooks Range pack growled low and deep, the rumble coming from more than the handful of wolves on the hill. The sound may not have been as strong or powerful as a Dire growl, but it certainly was nothing to scoff at.

Thin Man dropped his hands, looking fierce. "That's not your business."

"It is our business if you're holding Omega shewolves against their will," Luc said, already sure his offer would be rejected. "Show us your women, let us know they're safe and have autonomy to make their own decisions, and we'll leave."

The pack didn't respond, but twitchy Rudkin had grown visibly irritated. He'd also caught the eye of another male in his pack. Luc watched the two have a conversation without words, feeling the confidence grow between them. Knowing they had formulated some sort of plan. Thin Man wasn't the wolf to worry about—it was Rudkin and his friends.

Luc sent his senses further, dialed them up to an eight, to see if he'd missed something. Anything. The Dire mates were safe in the house—worried, but relatively calm—and alone. The only wolves he sensed were behind the hill—thirty from the Brooks Range pack stayed hidden in the trees and on the hill. No new pack, no surprises. Luc had faith in his brothers and their skills, knew they could take down a pack of thirty even with only the seven of them fighting.

Still, he worried. Something was coming from Rudkin and his subset. Something that Luc feared would upend the entire fight.

It didn't take long for Rudkin to show his hand. "I hear you've got a baby hidden away up there with your mates. How about you show us the little one, and then we'll think about letting you see our women." Rudkin glanced at his packmate, grinning. "Or maybe we'll just take the little bundle from you as payment for invading our home."

Thaus' roar shook the trees, his body morphing into a nightmare cross between his human self and his wolf side in the blink of an eye. The sudden rage, the total abandonment of patience and calm from the beastly Dire, infused Luc's power and sent it screaming out of him. There was no controlling it, no holding it back. Luc was broadcasting Thaus' anger across the range, and the pack on the other side of the valley took the brunt of it.

Instead of standing their ground and talking more, the Brooks Range pack—fueled by Thaus' energy running through Luc—attacked as one unit. The wolves poured over the hill, flooding the valley. Charging toward the hill and the Dires.

"Boss," Deus said, as if looking for permission to act.

Luc gave it. "No one gets up this hill."

And with that, his Dires raced down the incline, diving into battle with the Brooks Range pack. Luc's energy, his fervor, his unbridled rage that someone or something would threaten his family and his mate, cast itself outward, inflaming the fight. His brothers were particularly brutal in their fighting style—taking down two or three wolves at a time without mercy. Claws and teeth being put to work. Blood soon bathed the grasses around them, darkening the ground and creating a slippery condition the Brooks Range wolves simply couldn't find their balance in.

Luc didn't bother to join in the fight. He stood on his hill—the last wall of defense should anyone sneak past his brothers—and attempted to regain control of his senses, tried to pull everything back so he could calm the situation. Too late, it seemed. Already, the Brooks Range pack had begun their retreat, a handful of their members slipping off through the woods and racing away. Scattering. The rest... well, there were a lot of dead wolves in the valley. None of them Dires. There were also a handful of wolves still fighting, as if they had any hope of winning.

Luc's distraction from the fight started as a blip. An almost invisible pressure on his psyche coming at him from behind. A sense of movement that wasn't supposed to be there. He wouldn't have even noticed it, but the pressure created a slight void in its wake. Something he couldn't have looked for but was impossible not to notice once it had his attention. He lost his concentration, paying no mind to the retreating pack before him and only that blip. The one heading straight for the house where the women and baby waited for them.

Luc didn't even have time to growl, let alone speak. The realization that something had gotten around them and was heading for their Omegas came at the same time as a group of shifters broke off from the pack, shifted, and raced forward. His brothers shifted human as well, running straight into the renewed battle. All except for two—Thaus and Bez. Both stayed at the back of the fight, almost guarding Luc. Waiting to see if they'd even be needed.

Luc definitely needed them. As did Ariel and Micah.

"Thaus," Luc said, losing control of every bit of his own mind to the need to follow that blip. "Go. The house...the baby."

Thaus was running before Luc finished speaking, heading straight for the house. Bez followed him, racing hard after his brother. And Luc…

Luc was unable to resist the pull of the blip, the fear that his own mate might be in danger and he needed to protect her, for a single second.

Seventeen

Cassiel had never wanted to go home more than she did right then. Sadly, she had a feeling if she tried, the women she'd been cooped up with would stop her. Likely without breaking a sweat. They may have looked normal—otherworldly beautiful, though relatively average in terms of size—but Cassiel had already figured out that their brand of normal was simply…not.

She hugged Moxie a little closer, doing her best to keep all her dogs calm and controlled in the small space. Not an easy feat for sure, but no way was she letting them roam the house or go outside. If something dangerous had come to the Range, she needed to know what it was, how to fight it, and how to kill it. She needed her dogs safe, too.

And Luc. My god, how she worried about Luc. Even if he didn't deserve her attention right then.

"It'll be okay," a beautiful blond woman said as she came to sit beside Cassiel, even reaching out to pet Moxie's ears. "I know this seems really chaotic right now, but it's not the norm. The men will take care of things, and then we can all go back home."

Her voice remained soft and steady, and her movements were quite calm and oddly soothing—Cassiel had never seen anyone as polished and beautiful in real life. But she knew when someone was trying to convince her of something... and when they were trying to convince themselves.

"Chaotic is an understatement, and I have a feeling going home isn't going to be an option anytime soon for us." Cassiel shrugged, unable not to. Unable to keep her cool around predators. Beautiful and poised or not, these women were just like Luc. They were animals inside.

They were not to be trusted.

"I think she's got this situation pegged pretty well." Another woman—dark hair, golden skin, and with a bundle of blankets in her arms—padded closer, giving Cassiel a friendly smile before looking to the blonde.

"Charmaine, will you please hold Micah while I run to the bathroom?"

The blonde—Charmaine—lit up the room with her smile. "You never have to ask, Ariel. Give me that precious angel."

Charmaine, Ariel, Micah...angel names. Just like hers. Luc had called her angel a few times, too. Perhaps a coincidence. Perhaps not.

Cassiel waited for Ariel to leave the room before asking, "Who are all these women?"

Charmaine looked confused. "We are the mates of the men. Luc didn't explain our pack?"

As if. "Luc didn't explain anything about wolves or even tell me he was one, so no. No pack information was shared. Not any sort of information was shared. I simply mushed up onto your pack, thinking Luc might need help, and here I am." The lone human. Just her and her dogs and a pack of wolves.

Totally normal.

A woman with deep brown skin and short, cloud-like curly hair laughed from her place sitting against the opposite wall. "Sounds like Luc. The silent watchman." She stood and moved closer slowly, like how one would approach an injured dog. As if Cassiel was a threat. "I'm Michaela. You met Charmaine and Ariel. That freckle-faced cutie over there is Sariel. Momma-to-be is Amy, and the bitch with the glower in the corner is Zoe."

"I heard that," said the bitch with the glower in the corner. Who was actually glowering out the window. And not really glowering but looking worried. In fact, all the women looked worried. Not a good sign.

"You know I love you." Michaela sent Zoe an air kiss then shook her head. "We're all family here, Cassiel. All pack. We take care of one another."

But not her. She wasn't pack—she was just a girl too stupid to figure out the man who she'd thought was too good to be true really was. "I'd like to go home."

Michaela's smile fell, and she glanced toward Zoe. "Oh. Well…no one is keeping you here, but it's dangerous out there right now."

Zoe moved away from her post at the window, beelining for Ariel's side when she walked back into the room. "Until we know what the threat out there is, it's safest in here. With us."

Michaela patted Moxie's head. "How about you sit with us until everyone comes back, then we'll get you home?"

Cassiel took a deep breath, hugged Moxie closer, and voiced her greatest fear at that moment. "What if Luc won't let me leave?"

Six growls sounded in the room, upsetting her dogs. Every woman stared at her, all looking fierce and ready to fight, all so much more animal than human in that moment.

It was Ariel who spoke, baby back in her arms and eyes

lit with a fire Cassiel had never seen before. "No one will hold you against your will, Cassiel. If I can't guarantee that, my mate will. And Luc may be Alpha of this pack and the biggest Dire Wolf, but Thaus never loses a fight. He will fight for your freedom."

The other women all nodded, throwing their support into the mix. Their confidence, their willingness to fight for her right to leave, soothed something deep inside her. Something she hadn't even realized needing soothing. She had a posse of women at her side, ready to make sure she wasn't held against her will, ready to fight for her. And she had a feeling they weren't messing around about that.

She liked these chicks.

— —

Time crawled. As angry as Cassiel had been and as filled with fear as the wolves had made her, those emotions couldn't overpower the worry in her gut. The worry for Luc. Why she was so concerned about him, she wasn't sure, but she was. And she hated herself a little bit for that fact.

It didn't help that the women around her seemed worried, too. They had all grown quiet as the minutes had passed, more and more of them looping by the lone window to look outside. Sighing and walking away when they didn't see what they wanted to out there. Ariel and Charmaine had used the term mates, so Cassiel assumed the men were like husbands to the women. She understood that—the need to make sure the one you loved was safe. She definitely understood that.

And she really, really hoped Luc was okay out there, even if she was still mad at him.

It was a thump outside that brought all of them to their feet, the silence that ensued charged and deadly. The dogs all went stock-still, ears up and eyes locked on the same spot. Even the baby seemed tense, everyone in the room turning and staring at the door.

"I'll go," Michaela said, peeling herself away from Zoe and Ariel.

"I'm coming too." Sariel joined her, the two women creeping toward the door together.

Cassiel snapped her fingers for the dogs to follow her. "Might as well make it a party."

Michaela glanced down at the dogs and frowned at Cassiel. "This could get dangerous."

"I'm okay with danger," Cassiel said with a shrug, as if danger plopped its fat ass on her porch every day for a morning coffee. She shouldn't have been so casual, but she couldn't help it. Anything to move this party along so she could go home. But also, there was a baby and a pregnant woman in the room—no way could they fight. Cassiel believed in taking care of those weaker than yourself, so of course, she'd jump in to help.

Michaela finally nodded. "Fine. But if it's not one of the Dire men out there, I want you to shift."

"Shift what?"

The women all seemed to hold their breath, staring at Cassiel in a way that made her skin crawl. What the heck had just happened?

It was Michaela who jumped in with a question. "You don't know how to shift?"

Cassiel glanced around the room, feeling really, really stupid. "Sorry, but I have the same question—shift what?"

"Oh," Sariel said, looking at Ariel. "This makes so much more sense now."

"What does?"

But no one had time to answer because the dogs exploded into a cacophony of barks and growls, all focused on the door in front of Michaela. The woman jumped back just as the slab of wood was swung open.

By a child.

The tiny girl stood in a raggedy dress, filthy and way too skinny but with bright eyes that seemed to take in everything at once. Cassiel pushed the dogs behind her, shushing them, unsure if this little person was a threat or someone who needed protection. She edged toward the latter but didn't voice that opinion, letting everyone else regain their footing first. A child bursting through the door likely hadn't been something the women had been prepared for.

It was Amy—the quiet, pregnant one—who spoke first. "Are you okay, little one?"

The child darted a look her way, seemingly scared. Terrified, really. Cassiel wasn't sure whether she should help the kid or drop kick her out of the house. She'd seen horror movies—she knew how bad kids could be. Innocent-looking little packages of evil, some of them.

But the little one didn't attack or grin or say creepy things. Instead, she teared up, and she swallowed hard before she whispered, "I don't know if I'm okay, but I need help."

Loud bangs and growls sounded from behind her, making the little girl spin and squeal. Sariel jumped into action, picking up the child and clutching her against her chest. All the women—Cassiel and her dogs included—jumped in front of the child. Protecting the weakest.

"What's the threat?" A huge and downright vicious-looking man with no clothes on said as he hit the open door, beelining for Ariel and baby Micah. The man had to be her mate, Thaus. "Are you okay?"

Everyone froze again when the little one in Sariel's arms whimpered, obviously terrified of the hulking male stranger in their midst. Well, stranger to the child and Cassiel. He was pack to the rest of them. Family.

How they all weren't scared of him anyway, Cassiel might never know.

"Sariel." A light-eyed man with a soldier's stare stood in the doorway, also naked, looking toward the freckle-faced woman with the little girl on her hip. "Whose child is this, and where did she come from?"

Sariel turned, almost as if to protect the little girl from the man in the door. "We don't know. She just…showed up."

Luc appeared behind the light-eyed man, looking at Cassiel, breathing hard. As much as she wanted to deny it, Cassiel had never been more grateful to see someone in all her life. Luc was still alive, still whole, and still looking at her as if she mattered to him. Her heart actually thumped, and her body responded to his closeness. But his nakedness. Did none of these people believe in staying dressed?

Luc didn't seem bothered by his lack of clothing. "Are you okay?"

"Yeah." Cassiel stepped closer to Luc, the two coming together separate from the rest of the group. She rose onto the balls of her feet and whispered, "The little girl just showed up and said she doesn't know if she's okay. We have no idea who she is."

"We need to find out. A child shouldn't be alone in the woods like that. Not even one…" He paused, looking toward Sariel and the little girl. Frowning. "Like me."

Like him. Like someone who could turn into a giant predator. A wolf. "Is she like you?"

Luc shook his head, looking confused, unable to stop staring at the little girl. "I can't tell—"

Footsteps sounded on the stairs, and Luc spun, pushing Cassiel deeper into the room. Three men rushed inside, all naked, none familiar to her. They must not have been familiar to the other women either, because someone screamed. Luc, Light-eyes, and Ariel's mate jumped into action, fighting and snarling and being more violent than she'd ever seen someone be. The rage on Luc's face as he attacked the men, the harshness of his actions, made her blood run cold. These men were killers, plain and simple, and she needed to get away from them.

But there was nowhere to go.

Suddenly, a fourth man rushed into the room, which had dissolved into pure chaos. He headed straight for Cassiel, who had the unlucky privilege of being the one closest to the door. The man grabbed her by her throat before she could retreat, before she could scream. Her dogs, bless them, attacked en masse, all six of them biting, jumping, and snarling at the man as Cassiel grabbed the hands on her throat and tried to peel them away. She wasn't successful—in fact, she was pretty sure the only thing her embedding her nails into his hands did was piss him off.

The man growled in her face. "Don't even think of trying anything."

And then he kicked Moxie square in the ribs, the dog squealing in pain as she was thrown across the room.

"No," she gasped, unable to take in enough breath to scream. "Stop."

Luc spun, only just then noticing the added threat. He slashed at the man he'd been fighting with fingers that looked like claws, growling low as he stepped closer. As he hunched and glared at the man holding Cassiel.

"Let her go, Rudkin."

The man only increased the pressure on her throat, making her whimper. "Give me the child, and you can have her."

Luc shook his head, unable to catch Cassiel's eye. "That's not an option, but you need to take your hands off my mate."

The argument continued, but Cassiel could no longer hear the words being spoken. She could only stare at Luc, only had the energy to hold his gaze as something inside her responded to him. Something deep and dark and burning. A pulsing sort of energy built from her gut, a low growl rumbling up her chest. Shift, Michaela had said. And suddenly, Cassiel thought she might just have known what the woman had meant. Something not of her but inside of her wanted out, and she had a feeling she wouldn't be able to stop it. So she gave Luc the tiny nod that she could, and she closed her eyes. Preparing for her own little death. Assuming either this thing inside her or the man with his hands on her throat would kill her.

But it was Luc's voice that set her bones on fire.

"Cassiel, shift."

Eighteen

Luc had never felt as much fear course through him as in the moment when he'd seen Cassiel hanging from Rudkin's hand. Her soft, human form was so weak, so fragile against one of his kind—no way could she withstand the attack. So he'd done the only thing he could think of— he'd given her an Alpha order. Called to the wolf inside of her that she didn't even know about. Infused her with the power of his Dire lineage and his own strength and ordered her to shift.

The fates help him, he'd forced that on the poor woman with no warning.

But the distraction her slow, painful shift caused to Rudkin, the pure horror written over his face as he stared at her instead of at the men he'd been fighting, gave Luc enough time to attack. To set upon the man who'd erroneously put his hands on Luc's mate. The man who needed to die.

Luc partially shifted, bringing out his claws, relishing the feel of his teeth lengthening and filling his mouth with sharp points. Ones he put on display as he lunged at Rudkin while releasing a vicious snarl. There was no other warning for Rudkin before Luc had his claws deep in the man's neck. One swipe, one plunge with his claws, and the man dropped. He'd be dead in moments, once he bled out right there on the floor.

Cassiel still had not fully shifted forms, so she fell with her captor. Luc adjusted course mid-step, sliding his body forward as his mate finally completed her shift. He caught Cassiel's wolf—the tiny, light-colored beast barely bigger than one of her beloved sled dogs—as she fell toward the ground, punching with his other arm to push Rudkin's unconscious body away from her. The man could bleed out and die on that floor; Luc had more important things to worry about.

Still, his attention stayed split, a small part on the fight raging around them and the majority on Cassiel. His mate looked tired and weak, and Luc worried he'd have to stop fighting to shore her up, to herd her someplace out of the way and safe.

But Cassiel hadn't come to the homestead alone. With ears pricked and noses wriggling as they scented the little wolf of their owner, Cassiel's sled dogs approached. Slowly and with their heads low, they surrounded her. Supported her. Moxie even licked her ear as if to say *We know you.* Luc couldn't have asked for a better sign.

"Good dogs. Keep her safe," he said before diving full force into the battle. Six more of the Brooks Range pack men had joined the fray, and all of his Dire brothers were also there. The entire upper room had exploded into chaos that slowly leaked out the door and down the stairs, through the living space and out into the late evening light.

Even as Luc followed the fight out of the house, he kept his attention divided Kept watch on his Cassiel. Wobbly. That was the only way to describe her during those moments—like a newborn deer or lamb, she rocked and stumbled, her legs looking ready to collapse under the pressure of supporting her weight. But she was there. She was outside with her pack of dogs still taking care of her. She was also beautiful and worth fighting for.

Luc dispatched two more of the pack wolves—nearly beheading one who'd tried to rush past him toward where the women had stationed themselves—before realizing that the pack had been decimated. Only one Brooks Range member remained—a short, thick man with long dark hair and more attitude than sense.

"I'm not telling you nothing."

Phego sighed as he held the man on the ground. "I do so hate a double negative."

Luc almost laughed. "Find out what we need to know."

His Dire brother—the one trained in a ridiculous number of methods to torture shifters and humans alike—shot him an arrogant look. "You don't have to worry about that. I'll get what we need."

Of that, Luc had no doubt. He left Phego to his job as torturer and information-gatherer, heading straight for Cassiel.

"Are you okay, angel?"

The wolf didn't meet his gaze, her dark eyes locked on the ground at his feet instead. She was far from okay, but she seemed to be dealing. Luc couldn't really expect more than that, but Phego was about to get to work. Things would likely get a little worse once he did.

Luc knelt before Cassiel, patting each of her dogs—all of whom had stayed right by her side during the fight—before asking, "Will you let me guard you? I really don't want you to have to see what my brother is about to do."

Cassiel made no sound. Luc waited on his knees for

her, ready to be rejected but hoping for some sort of sign. It came in a single paw stepping forward. Then another. And another. Soon enough, he was able to sit on the ground and take the wolf in his lap. To wrap all that soft fur in his arms and stroke his hand along her spine to calm her. To calm himself too.

She was just so small.

"Your wolf has always been inside you," he whispered, nuzzling into the fur on her neck. "She is a part of you but has been neglected for so long. I'm sorry I forced you to shift, but I couldn't stand the thought of you getting hurt in the fight. Your human side is much weaker than your wolf one. Slower, too."

Cassiel perked up at that, her ears straightening and her head cocking. Luc would have laughed, but the sounds of Phego doing his job behind him definitely weren't funny.

"Come, sweet angel. Rest your head against my chest."

She pulled back as if wanting to look over his shoulder, her body stiffening at the sounds slowly building from behind them.

"This isn't what you think—those other men, those shifters, had a sickness. Something dark and dangerous building around them and spoiling the whole area. I've been following them for a long time, and they've been in a lot of trouble." Luc felt her body relax under his hand, so he resumed stroking her back. "When I first met them, I sensed the feminine spirits of two women with them. I no longer do, and I'm afraid that they've squirreled the women away somewhere against their will. That's why Phego is doing what he's doing. We have to save those women if they're even still alive."

The sound of a bone breaking preceded a scream that made Cassiel shake. Luc needed to distract her, so he did the only thing he could think of—he spoke.

"I was born centuries ago on another continent, in a country that no longer exists. I was raised in a pack but eventually left it and found my brothers. All of us—the men—we're Dire Wolves, an ancient breed with very few members alive anymore. We used to think we were the only seven left, but we have intel that there may be more in Australia."

Cassiel curled closer, fitting herself against his chest. Warming him literally and figuratively. That was a sign of trust, a move of acceptance. That was progress.

"We Dire Wolves fight on behalf of the president of the National Association of the Lycan Brotherhood, the ruling party over wolf shifters in the United States. We handle missions for him when there are no other options but for us to go in. The women here, like you, are Omega wolves—powerful in their own right. They are a true gift to the fates. We Dires were alone for most of our very long lives, and then Bez met Sariel while on a mission. Then Levi met Amy. Slowly, each of my brothers found their mates. They fought for them." Luc leaned closer. "Just as I will fight for you, my angel."

Before Luc could register any sort of reaction from Cassiel, Phego stole this attention with a quiet, "Luc, it's time."

Luc glided his hand over Cassiel's fur one last time. "I need to handle this in case the man has any info on where the women are. Stay with your dogs—they seem to be taking care of you."

"She's got us too," Michaela said, standing behind the sled dogs with Zoe and Charmaine beside her. "We won't let anything happen to her."

Their Omegas were fighting hard for one another. The very thought warmed him.

"Thank you for that, Omegas. We are truly blessed to have you in our pack." Luc headed to where Phego stood over the shifter who appeared to be missing some skin. A lot of skin. He couldn't think about that, though. "Where are the women?"

"Please," the man said, a gurgle sounding from inside his chest. "Kill me. Just kill me."

"Not until I know where the women are."

The man rocked his head from side to side, smearing blood on the grass below him. "No women—"

"Bullshit. I sensed them. I know you had women in your pack."

"Dead. Both dead…but the girls…"

Luc's heart dropped right there, the puzzle of this pack exploding into place. Girls—young ones. Children didn't come into their full gender identity until puberty, so of course he couldn't sense them. Same with the little girl who'd shown up at the cabin, the one Sariel was still caring for inside. He'd sensed no feminine power from her because she was too young to have grown into it. The pack didn't have women squirreled away, likely against their will—they had little girls. No wonder the Brooks Range wolves had taken on a sickness—acts against children were a crime against the fates. An unforgivable act. An atrocity.

Luc's inner wolf roared, ready to fight. Ready to kill. But first—

"Where are they?" He kicked the man in the side, his growl deep and thunderous. "Where are the children?"

The man shook his head, fading. Bleeding out.

"Seconds left," Phego said, watching placidly as if this was something he did every day. As if skinning a man alive and letting him bleed out was normal. And perhaps it was— shifters were hard to kill after all.

Luc crouched down so he could own the man's field of vision. "One more answer, and you can die. Tell me where the girls are, and you're done here."

The man nodded, just once, before he said, "The caves."

And then he was dead.

Luc searched his mind, his memories of his time spent in the Brooks Range flashing through his head. Caves? They'd already searched out the ones nearby, but that meant nothing, really. There were mountains and hillsides all over the place. There could be hundreds of caves big enough to live in. Searching them all could take them years. Time they didn't have.

"Get Sariel out here," he grumbled, rising to his feet. "Now. And bring the girl."

Bez walked out with his mate, who held the child as if Luc was a threat to them. Something that had not been his intention.

"Please," he said, giving the Omega her space so she could relax. "He said girls—plural—and that they are in the caves. Please, does the little one have any information about where she's been held or who was with her?"

Sariel kept her eyes on Luc's as she leaned down to whisper to the child. The girl turned in her arms, pinning Luc with a look. So very brave and strong.

"Gavreel is back there. Tabriss, too."

Three. Three children, two of whom were still in danger.

"Do you know how to get back to the cave? Can you take us there?"

The little girl's lip quivered, and she shook her head. "Woods. There was a lot of woods. I don't remember which direction."

Luc sighed, his hope for an easy search smashed. "Thank you—"

"Dina," Sariel said, filling in the gap for him. "This precious baby is Dina."

"Thank you, Dina. Why don't you go inside with Sariel and get something to eat?" Luc held it together until the child was back inside, until Ariel and Thaus had joined them with the baby. Until he couldn't control his anger anymore.

And then he let go.

All of his power, all of his rage, exploded into the atmosphere, feeding the universe with negativity and anger. He roared to the heavens, wanting to know so badly why the fates would burden him with such a task when he couldn't handle it. If those girls died, if he couldn't find them, that knowledge would destroy him. He knew it, his pack knew it, which was why his brothers said nothing as he screamed at the sky above them all.

But Cassiel didn't give him space. She rubbed her body along his legs, grounding him just enough to come back from the edge of insanity. Giving him a goal to run toward. He finally fell to the ground, pulling her into his lap once more. Burying his face in her fur.

"What if I can't find them?" He shook his head, that rage building again. "What if I take too long? I've been searching for these women for years, but they were already dead. What if my delays cost these girls their lives?"

Cassiel whimpered, rubbing her head against his. Comforting him when no comfort was deserved. He'd failed those little girls. All this time, all the hunting he'd done, and he hadn't even known they existed. He'd been looking for women—a shortsighted mistake on his point. One that could cost those little ones their lives.

"We'll find them," Deus said, his mate Zoe at his side. Both looking determined but fearful. Doubtful. "We have to find them."

"What caves, though?" Bez asked, sounding far more irritated than normal. "We're in the fucking mountains. There could be caves all over."

Cassiel hopped out of Luc's lap and yipped. Then yipped again. She growled at him and grabbed his hand in her mouth before pulling as if to drag him to his feet.

"What, angel?" he asked, staring at her as she bounced and growled. She'd figured out how to use her legs, that was for sure. "What do you want?"

"I think she wants to shift back to her human form," Zoe said, staring at the dog. Cassiel yipped and ran to bump into Zoe's legs then came back to Luc and yipped again. "Yeah, definitely. Make her shift."

Luc patted Cassiel's head again. "Are you sure you're ready?"

She full out barked, the woof sound deeper than he'd expected. Firmer. Cassiel wasn't playing around.

"Okay then." Luc rose to his feet, keeping his eyes locked on her little wolfy body. Letting the Alpha power within him build. Letting it grow until it was strong enough to take over someone else's free will. Until he knew he could make Cassiel do anything he wanted with nothing but his words.

"Cassiel, shift."

The shift was faster this time, still painful-looking, though. Luc grimaced as her human flesh re-covered her wolf fur, as every pale curve came back into being. But then she was there—fully shifted. And naked. So very naked. Luc definitely didn't mind, but she would.

Her breaths sounded harsh, and her arms shook as she pushed herself off the forest floor. "I...don't like that."

Luc could only smile. "It's hard the first few times."

Zoe appeared behind Cassiel and wrapped a cloak around her shoulders, covering her nakedness from the rest of their pack, as the woman rose to her feet. Cassiel glanced over her shoulder then tugged the fabric around her.

"Where are my clothes?"

Luc waved a hand over his own naked body. "They don't make the transition."

Moxie jumped at Cassiel, and his mate grinned as she patted the dog's head. "Are you ready for a run, girl?"

Luc's heart dropped a little. "A run?"

"Yeah." Cassiel threw herself into motion, hurrying across the muddy grass and grabbing harnesses from the seat of her sled. "I'm going to need something to wear to drive the sled."

Everyone froze, all eyes swinging to Luc. Cassiel was leaving. Sledding away from him and back into the wilderness. He had failed her, just as he would fail those children in the caves.

"Whatever you need," Luc said, his voice dead even to his own ears. His eyes dropping once he caught his pack's pitying gazes. "You are free to go. Michaela, if you could find her some clothes for the journey, please."

"Of course," the woman said, disappearing into the house.

"And Bez—perhaps you can run alongside Cassiel. Make sure she gets home safely." Because he had a feeling that—if she was leaving—she didn't want him following her. He would respect her wishes.

But Cassiel took him completely by surprise.

"Home? I'm not going home." She hooked the first two dogs to the sled before Michaela came out with a bundle of clothes. "Thanks. These should work. Whoever's coming along might want to throw some supplies in the sled as well."

"Coming along where?" Luc asked, daring to step closer. Hope filling up his empty chest.

"To the caves, of course. We need to find those girls. Now."

There was a moment when her words didn't make sense, when he couldn't understand the language he'd learned so long ago. But once they fell into place, a feeling of complete peace filled him.

"You're staying to help?"

Cassiel stopped messing with her dogs, staring at him for a long moment. Then she was in motion, running and diving into his arms. Wrapping him in her warmth and heat.

"They're in trouble, so yeah. I'm staying to help." She pulled back a little, just enough to put space between them so she could look into his eyes. "Besides, I have a feeling you need me to stick around. So, I'm here."

"You don't hate me?"

She shook her head, the motion slow. Deliberate. "No, though I need more information from you."

"Anything you want, it's yours."

"Good." She popped a quick kiss to his lips. "Then I want some supplies to take with us and a group to head to the caves. There may be hundreds of little caverns around the mountain, but I know of a few that are huge. If I were looking for a den protected from the elements, that's where I'd go."

"You are brilliant."

She grinned. "I know. It's going to get dark soon, but I have to imagine you wolves can see at night, yeah?"

"Of course."

"Good. Then let's get this party rolling."

Bez came down the steps from the porch. "You really think you know where these caves are?"

Cassiel winked at Luc before shooting Bez the most sarcastic expression known to man. "I've lived in the bush for most of my life, have been all over these mountains for years. This is my land, so I really only have one answer for you."

"What's that?"

"Duh." Her grin exploded over her face, her confidence soaring. "I'm the best bet to find them right now, so let's go."

Nineteen

The cold, evening air of the Brooks Range tasted sweeter than normal as Cassiel and her team cut paths through the woods and toward the natural caves on the north side of the mountain. Whatever sickness and sense of dread she'd been feeling lately were gone. Perhaps because the pack was dead. Perhaps because she had finally come to accept a part of herself she hadn't known existed. Perhaps because she had Luc running at her side.

She was a wolf. Plain and simple, no way around it—a wolf. Living inside her was what she had always feared. Though, maybe…

"Do you think the wolf that came to my room was like you…and me?" She looked over to the running Luc, whose big head bobbed up and down in an exaggerated sort of positive answer. "Yeah, I'm thinking that too. All these years, I was so afraid of that vision, but now I'm wondering if they were coming to find me or looking out for me or something. There have always been wolves in my life."

"We know our kind," Sariel said from the basket of the sled where she sat with the little girl in her lap. Luc had wrapped the two in blankets before they'd taken off, welcoming Dina into their fold and promising they'd figure something out to make sure she was properly cared for. Cassiel doubted there would be much figuring going on—Sariel seemed to have called dibs, and Dina might as well have been a koala baby, what with the way she clung to the woman. They definitely seemed to be a match.

Sariel turned, catching Cassiel's eye. "Have you ever noticed humans being a bit cautious around you?"

Cassiel laughed. "Well, sure, but I was the messed-up foster kid and, later, the crazy lady in the woods. I make people uncomfortable."

"It could have been your wolf. Charmaine looks like a model but can scare a human without even trying. I fit the stay-at-home-mom persona pretty well, but I've had people cross streets to avoid walking near me. Every now and then, humans can sense the predator within, and they don't like it."

That got Cassiel thinking about her past, about being tossed from home to home as a child, about all the people along the way who had tried to intimidate, overpower, or simply run away from her. Maybe she hadn't been the problem after all.

The dogs slowed, barking wildly as they raced over the soupy ground. They still had a ways to go, but there was no path out there, no way to move through the mud without struggle. This would be an exhausting journey for Cassiel's babies.

"Whoa, stop. Stop, Moxie." Cassiel stepped off the runners as soon as the dogs stopped, checking each one to make sure their feet were okay. Luc crept up beside her, bumping her hip as if asking what was wrong. "There's no path here, so they have to cut a trail. It's hard work, and I don't want them getting hurt doing it, so I need to make sure their paws and legs are okay."

Luc growled softly, making a whining sound at the end. Not that Cassiel had any idea what that all meant.

"I don't speak wolf, you know."

Suddenly, a very naked Luc stood beside her, wrapping Cassiel in his arms as if to blanket her. Something she appreciated.

"What can we do to help?" Luc asked, his voice a rough and grumbly vibration against her. One that called to the beast inside her, that made her heart jump, made her crave even more contact. One she didn't have time to think about right then.

"Unless you can cut a trail through all this underbrush, not a whole heck of a lot."

Luc looked ahead, then back at his wolf pack, then ahead of them again. "Shouldn't be a problem."

He shifted back to his wolf and ran ahead of her dogs, who definitely wanted to play *chase the wild animal*. The other wolves who'd come with them—Bez, Mammon, Charmaine, Deus, and Zoe—followed Luc, cutting one heck of a trail with their big bodies.

"Welp, guess I should have figured that out earlier."

Sariel laughed. "This is all new to us. We don't usually run with dogs."

"Can I run with them?" Dina asked, looking up at Sariel with a smile.

The woman practically melted right there. "Maybe on the way back, little one. We need you rested to help us in the caves."

Dina settled against Sariel's chest, still smiling. "Gav and Tabby will be happy to see us."

Sariel shot Cassiel a look. One filled with fear and worry—they'd be happy to see the Dire Wolves…if they were still alive. And if the pack could find them. All things still up in the air at the moment.

Not that Sariel would admit that to a child. "I sure hope so."

Cassiel mushed on, the ride easier and the dogs happier with a path to follow and other animals to chase. She also watched Luc lead the big, scary wolves through the forest. He was definitely the biggest of the group, with almost black fur and silver spots over his back. He ran with a grace to his stride, an athleticism that challenged even his fellow wolves. Cassiel liked watching him run. She liked watching him, period. There was an attraction there for sure, a bond she had never experienced. He'd called her his mate, but what that meant to her, she wasn't sure yet.

She was pretty sure she wanted to find out, though

They arrived at the entrance to the cave system as the light finally began to fade from the region. Twenty hours of sunlight had never been enough for her, but perhaps the knowledge of what she could become—learning more about the predator that she was—would ease her fears. Not yet, though. Cassiel shivered as the shadows grew deeper, doing her best to smile at all the naked people as she handed them the bundles of fabric they'd brought so they could cover themselves. Thankful when Luc—already wearing the brown cloak she'd handed him—came up behind her and pulled her into his arms.

"You okay?"

"Yeah, I just...it's getting dark."

He hummed, cradling her. "You're not prey anymore, Cassiel. You're the predator."

She spun in his arms, reaching up to hold on to his shoulders. "A predator with a mate."

His growl was dark, deep, and fierce, as was the kiss he planted on her lips. He obviously liked her using that word.

"Okay, you two," Zoe yelled, lined up outside the

entrance with the others. "Let's cut out the PG-13 show. We have children to find."

Cassiel felt her cheeks burning brightly as she pulled away. "Oops."

"It's to be expected," Luc said, still clinging to her. "The need to be close is only going to get worse."

"It will?"

"Of course. The mating imperative..." He stopped, staring down at her with a furrowed brow. "I keep forgetting all of this is new for you."

"New and completely confusing."

"It's okay. I'll slow down. You can ask me anything you want to as well."

"Cool because we're about to spend some serious time together under a mountain." Cassiel headed toward the entrance, raising her voice so the others could hear her once she reached them. "There are three options once we get inside. All three I'd say are big enough and go deep enough for someone to have hidden children away in, so it's not like we can choose to ignore one of them."

Bez nodded. "So we need to split up."

"Definitely."

Luc jumped right in. "Deus and Zoe will take one path, Mammon and Charmaine another, and Cassiel and I the third. Bez, you and Sariel remain out here with Dina. If we feel the need to bring the child inside, we will, but I'd really prefer not to."

"Understood." Bez turned and headed for the sled where Sariel seemed to be playing a patty-cake game with the little girl.

"She's not going to let the child go," Cassiel said, keeping her voice low so hopefully only Luc could hear her.

"And maybe that's just what Dina needs."

And Gavreel. And Tabriss. The two little ones still stuck inside the caves.

Luc must have known where Cassiel's thoughts had gone. "You ready?"

"As ready as I'll ever be." She moved toward the rest of the pack, turning on the headband flashlight she'd brought with her and handing out the two others. "Stay together, be careful, and if anything seems or feels off, backtrack. These caves are old, and I have no idea how stable anything is inside there."

Cassiel led the way into the caves with Luc on her heels and the rest of the crew behind him. The temperature of the air dropped significantly inside the darkness, the air developing a moist and weighty feel to it. Cassiel shivered in the cold, wondering how the little girls had fared inside. Had stayed warm and comfortable without the sun to feed them. Her fear for them—and her anger at the people who had held them—grew with every step.

When they made it to the split, she stopped, nodding to Luc to make the next decision.

"Mammon and Charmaine, go right. Deus and Zoe, center. I'll go with Cassiel to the left. We meet at the entrance in thirty minutes whether we find anything or not."

The men grasped forearms, looking like some sort of superhero group to Cassiel. When they broke apart, each team of two started down their respective paths, Luc watching them go and looking so very worried.

"You really care about them."

Luc turned, his eyes shadowed in the dark around them. "They're my pack, my brothers. Yes, I worry about them." He stepped closer, crowding her. "I worry about you too."

Cassiel huffed, moving into the cave and away from the man who said things that made her heart flutter. "I'm fine. I've also been on my own for a long time, so there's no need to worry about me."

"You're strong and independent, but there's so much

need within you. My beautiful angel wants more than she has."

Cassiel froze, unable to move another step. "What are you talking about?"

"I can feel things—sense people. My pack is strongest, but other people's emotions show up as well. This pack in the woods—they've been dragging me into a sort of funk because of the sickness within them. That's been very hard to deal with."

"Do all wolves have this power?"

"No. Just me, as far as I know."

"Oh." She turned to face him, shining the light on him in the process. "Is that why you showed up at my house all crazed and out of it?"

Luc nodded. "We were hunting the pack."

"Why?"

"They were sick—I could feel it. Also, I'd sensed feminine energy at one point, but then that disappeared. They claimed to be holding two females, and I worried it was against the women's wishes. They also tried to take Zoe hostage."

"They what? How were any of them left standing?"

Luc chuckled. "Yes, she's quite the spitfire. She and Deus managed to run the pack off, but that bad energy over the Range just grew and grew. I've been up here for years, slowly going insane trying to figure out what the pack was doing."

"Kidnapping children, apparently."

"Or breeding females for them."

Cassiel shivered. "They sound pleasant."

"Hence why we killed them."

"Did you really just use hence?"

"Yes. Why?"

"It's an old-man word."

"I am an old man."

"How old?"

"They didn't track birthdays the way they do today when I was born. The closest guess I have is around two thousand years."

Cassiel stopped, staring at him. Unable to form words as his knocked around in her brain. "You're what?"

"Shifters live a long time—Dire Wolves, specifically."

"So all the wolves in your…"

"My pack?"

"Yes."

"They're not all as old as me, but most of the men are at least a thousand years old. The women are more in their early hundreds."

"Early hundreds." She nodded, rocking her head slowly up and down as if that would help make sense of the words. "You're really selling this whole 'be a shifter' thing. Except for the whole raping women part. I could skip all of that."

Luc's growl echoed throughout the cave. "That won't happen to you. I would die first."

Cassiel melted a little, the strength and conviction behind his words warming her from the inside. "You're sweet. Scary, but sweet."

"I've never been called sweet before, so thank you."

"You get called scary a lot?"

"All the time."

"I can see that," Cassiel said, moving deeper into the cavern. Back on the hunt. "So, tell me more. What's life as a wolf like?"

And so they spent the next twenty minutes, him talking to her in a soothing sort of voice, filling in the details that would help her transition from human to wolf shifter. On things like instincts and longevity, healing abilities and strength. On what would happen if she embraced her inner wolf and let the beast have some control of her. How amazing it was to have the two sides working in concert.

Cassiel wasn't convinced.

"It's just so unusual," she said as they turned another corner in their crazy, stone tunnel.

"I'm sure it is for you, thinking you were human all these years, then finding out that's only partially true. That's not the way most shifters develop."

"Apparently I'm not most shifters."

"No, my angel. You are not."

"Why do you call me that?"

"Angel?"

"Yes. I noticed all the other women in your group have angel names as well." Cassiel frowned. "Except Amy."

Luc chuckled. "If it helps you complete your puzzle, her real name is Armaita."

"Ah, that makes sense now." Cassiel kept moving and thinking, unable to stop her mind from spinning. "Even these little girls—angel names. Why is that?"

"Because you're all Omega shewolves."

Shewolf, she understood—Omega? "So, not only am I a wolf shifter, I'm a special wolf shifter?"

"Technically…yes. Omegas are always females, full of a power that is considered a gift to their packs, and we believe them to be descendants of the extinct Dire Wolf breed."

"You're not extinct."

"Not yet, but close. Even if there are more of us on earth than my seven—which I only somewhat believe could be a possibility—there couldn't be many. We're too obvious in wolf form to be hidden without a lot of effort."

"Because of your spots?"

Luc stopped, his voice giving away his surprise. "You noticed?"

"I had a dog with ermine spots once. I was fascinated by them. Yours are silver, though. Very striking against your dark fur and, yes, impossible to hide."

There was a long silence as Luc stood frozen, staring at Cassiel with a shocked expression on his face. At least until he huffed what sounded a lot like a laugh. "You surprise me more and more, Cassiel."

"And you worry me." Cassiel stopped again, the trek obviously sidetracked. Her heart pounding in her chest. "I don't know if I can accept all of this."

"All of what?"

"The wolf thing, which seems like I sort of don't have a choice in. But also you, your pack, the whole—" she waved a hand between them "—mating hullabaloo. I barely know you."

Luc stared at her for a long moment before nodding once. "It is a lot, but please know I would never force myself on you in any way. If you told me to leave you alone, I would."

Doubt had never tasted so strong. "But would you really?"

He paused, watching her. Likely weighing his answer. "I'd keep watch, but you'd never see me again. Unless you called to me. Or you needed my help."

"So, you're stuck with me?"

"No. I'm blessed to have you. I believe you being stuck with me is the drawback in this situation."

"And if we don't get along? If we argue a lot?"

Luc pulled her in close, hugging her tightly. "Then we argue. Couples argue, from what I understand of this modern world."

"Yes, they do…but most couples don't have claws. We do."

"I promise not to get mad if you use them against me."

Cassiel choked on a snort. "And my teeth? What about those?"

Luc leaned close, silent. His stare blazing. The air growing thick and warm between them. The mood shifting fast. He brushed his lips against hers as he whispered, "You can bite me anytime you want. It's how we finalize our mating. I'm quite looking forward to the feel of you tasting me, in fact."

Oh. "You want me to bite you?"

Luc shivered, growling low and pulling her close. "I do, but only when you're ready. There's no coming back from that level of bonding. You'd never be able to get rid of me."

Cassiel didn't think that was such a bad idea, so instead of pulling away, she kissed him, tangling herself in his scent and his touch. Forgetting all of their responsibilities and the needs of others around them. At least until she heard shouting from behind them.

"Luc. Cassiel. We found them."

Twenty

The absolute joy of having his mate in his arms came to a cold, hard stop as soon as he heard those words yelled through the cave. The girls had been found, and if the tone of Deus' voice was any indication, they were alive.

"They found them," he said, trying hard to rationalize those words.

"And the voice sounded positive," Cassiel said, obviously on the same thought path as Luc. "Hopefully they're okay."

But Luc already knew they were—he could sense the relief of his pack, the absolute rage of Bez, tempered by the love of Sariel. Those girls were alive—likely neglected or in some sort of bad shape, but alive. And his pack would never let anything happen to them again. Period.

"Come on." Cassiel grabbed his hand, tugging him with her. "Let's go meet them and see what they need from us."

Luc went along willingly, hanging on to his mate's warm hand as if dropping it would sever his lifeline. And maybe it would—she'd helped them find the girls, had alleviated the worst stress he'd ever experienced in his very long life, and quieted the world when he needed it. Cassiel was his own personal angel, and he couldn't imagine letting go of her. Ever.

Still, Luc tried his hardest to focus on what needed to be done, to push off the mating imperative for the moment. The little girls had to take priority. Once they were examined by Michaela and Ariel and received whatever care they needed, he could shift his focus to his mate.

He already knew the girls were going to have an amazing home with his pack if they needed one. Sariel would be thrilled to have two more little ones to care for.

It took far longer than either of them would have liked to find the mouth of the cave, but eventually, they made it out of the darkness and into the night. Sariel stood by the sled with the three little girls crowded around her, all looking raggedy and so very underfed. Luc's wolf roared for them—for the fact that someone could treat them so poorly. Little angels who deserved to be loved and cared for had been left in the dark of the caves for…shit, he had no idea. Likely years if his own senses had been accurate over his time in Alaska.

Bez moved close to Luc as soon as he and Cassiel exited the cave. "My mate is very protective of the girls."

Luc could see that with his own eyes and feel the connections between the motherly Omega shewolf and all three of the girls growing with every second. Sariel had always been meant to be a mother, but her body made having her own children an impossibility. She'd raised sweet Angelina, an Omega Bez had rescued along with Sariel, but she'd been a teenager in human years at that point. These girls were much younger. And they definitely favored Sariel.

"I assumed she would be," Luc said, holding tight to Cassiel. Gauging the comfortableness of the girls before taking a single step in their direction.

But Bez wasn't finished. "She's going to want to—"

"I know." Luc patted his friend, his brother, on the shoulder. "I'll take care of what I can."

Luc approached the girls slowly, bringing Cassiel with him, dropping to his knees in front of the little ones so as not to scare them.

"Which of you ladies is Gavreel?"

The little girl on the left raised her hand, her deep green eyes locked on his. So brave, that little shewolf. "I am, sir."

Sir. He didn't deserve the title.

"And so this is Tabriss." Luc nodded toward the redhead on the right. "The three Musketeers, reunited. Are you okay? Do you need anything right now?"

All three turned to look at Sariel, who stood protectively over them. When she smiled, they shook their heads in unison.

"Don't be afraid to ask us for anything," Luc said, guessing the girls' shyness might override their basic needs for comfort and security. They definitely seemed on edge, and he had a feeling his next question was only going to make that worse. "Do you know where your parents are?"

"Our moms are dead," Gavreel said, her face unchanging. Her voice flat and unemotional. "They died in the caves a long time ago. Dina doesn't even remember hers."

Little Dina shook her head, looking so damn heartbroken and sad. And tiny. By the fates, were the girls small.

"And your dads?" Luc hated asking, knowing the likelihood of how these gifts had been brought into the world. Of how much of a nightmare their moms must have lived.

Gavreel didn't falter, though. "We were never told who our fathers were."

Of course not, because the children hadn't been born from a normal sort of union. But that was the end of what Luc needed to know. There was no use putting the children through more at that moment. They could ask for more at a later time, when the girls had had a chance to adjust to living outside the Brooks Range pack. Because no way were they leaving them behind.

"You three are very brave and strong. I hope you know that."

Gavreel—while obviously the leader of the group—nodded toward the smallest one. "Dina is the brave one. She decided to run because the men scared her. I tried last year but couldn't find my way out."

Luc reached for the little Omega, holding his hand flat and still to allow her time to accept his offer. When she did—when she mimicked his movements and touched his fingers with hers—his heart skipped two beats. "You are a warrior, little Dina. Never forget that."

She nodded, tucking her head against Sariel's stomach as if to hide. A warrior in what looked to be a raggedy nightgown and bare feet, who'd run all the way to—

"Did you shift?" Luc asked Dina as pieces of the puzzle became clearer. "When you ran out of the cave, were you in human or wolf form?"

"Wolf. I'm faster that way."

So she could already shift. But when he had arrived at the house, she'd been wearing that same nightgown. "Did you carry your clothes with you?"

Dina shook her head, glancing toward Gavreel, who jumped in to answer the unspoken question.

"She can shift and her clothes end up with her. The bad men were fascinated by it and would make her shift a lot."

Holy hell. That—shifting and bringing your clothes with you through forms—simply didn't happen. Little Dina was a special Omega, indeed.

Or perhaps not an Omega at all.

"The shifting hurt," Dina said, sounding sad but with a

little edge to her voice. A little attitude. "The bad men were mean and didn't listen when I said I wanted to stop."

Tabriss grabbed Dina's shoulder, frowning. "She would cry," she said, the lilt in her words indicating she had likely grown up somewhere much farther south than where they were. "She shouldn't have to shift so much."

"And she won't have to again," Sariel said, bringing little redheaded Tabriss closer. "We would never force a child to endure something so stressful."

"Sariel is right," Luc said, glancing up at Sariel. "Now, what do you think about going home?"

Dina's bottom lip trembled. "I don't want to live in the caves anymore."

"Oh no," Sariel said, scooping the little girl up in her arms. "No caves, my love. Homes. Real homes with beds and toys and food. Would you like that?"

Dina looked down to her two partners in crime before nodding, all three girls moving closer to Sariel. The Omega brought her gaze to Luc, striking him with a ferocious sort of stare that said more than words ever could. No fucking way was she leaving without these girls.

"We have a homestead not too far away, which is where Dina found us. Right now, we all live together as a pack right here in Alaska, and we're strong. We'll keep you safe, and no one from our pack will harm you." Luc rose to his feet and nodded at Sariel. "Load them up into the sled. We'll take them back with us."

Sariel seemed to relax. "Thank you."

There was no need to thank him, but he nodded anyway, leaning into Cassiel to steal a little comfort from having her close. She wrapped her arms around his waist and held him tightly, likely doing the same. A thought that lit up his insides.

But there was still work to do.

"We run home," Luc said, raising his voice so all of his pack knew his intentions. "Bez, take the lead. Sariel will ride with the girls, and Cassiel will handle the sled. We are their protectors. Their guards. And no one stops that sled until they are safely on Dire property. Period."

His pack nodded, all of them looking fierce and ready to fight. Ready to defend their own. Because those three little girls didn't know it yet, but they'd just been adopted by the Dire Wolf pack. And no one fucked with a Dire and lived to tell the tale.

"Luc," Bez said quietly, tugging him away from his mate who walked off to ready her sled. "Sariel is already attached to the children."

Luc knew where this was going and what Bez was likely about to ask of him. It was a question that didn't need to be voiced, though. "I hope you have enough bedrooms down there in Texas."

Bez glanced at his mate, love and fierce protectiveness flaring there. "I'll build them a fucking princess tower if that's what they want. Anything to make Sariel and those girls happy."

Luc patted him on the shoulder. "Good man."

"So, you're staying in Alaska?" Bez asked, nodding toward Cassiel, who had the dogs turned around and was helping Sariel get the girls settled.

That was an easy answer. "I'm going wherever she does."

Bez chuckled. "Never thought I'd see the day."

"I believe I said that to you a while back."

"You did, so we've come full circle."

"All good stories must." Luc left his friend and brother to shift and headed to his mate. To the one woman he would do anything for. To his perfect match. "You ready to go?"

She nodded but seemed edgy. Off.

Luc wasn't about to let that go. "What's wrong?"

Cassiel glanced at the girls in the sled then grabbed Luc's arm and pulled him away. "What if they come back?"

"Who?"

"The pack. The ones who had the girls. What if there are more of them, and they come to collect these little ones?"

Luc's growl broke the stillness of the night. "They'll not survive if they try to take those girls from us."

Cassiel looked over her dogs, still frowning. "So, I should just keep going? No matter what happens along the way?"

"Yes. No matter what, you keep driving the girls to the homestead. Thaus, Phego, and Levi will be there to jump into a fight if they need to."

"And where will you be?"

"I'll stay about twenty yards behind so nothing sneaks up on you."

Cassiel snuggled into his chest. "I have to admit, I'm a little uncomfortable with the thought of you not running beside me."

Luc's heart pounded harder, his body warming. These were all good signs from his mate—hints that maybe, just maybe, she would someday accept him as her chosen mate. He certainly hoped she would, at least.

"No one will hurt you, my angel. I won't let it happen." Luc leaned down and kissed her nose, unable not to take an extra deep sniff of her scent before pulling back. "Besides, your wolf is awake now. She'll help you if you need her to."

"What if she's too weak? What if I don't know how to access her?"

"You won't have to worry about that."

"How do you know?"

Luc kissed her deeply, a rumble sounding from deep within him. Loving the way he felt her body respond to his, before pulling away. "Shall I call her forward, my angel? Do you want me to remind you of the beautiful beast within?"

Cassiel nodded, holding on to his arms. Luc kissed her one last time before growling low while staring into her eyes, letting his wolf come forward. Inviting hers to come out and play. He sensed the spirit within her, the weakness of that presence, but the wolf was there. She would grow stronger with every shift. Luc would make sure of it.

It was a single moment, a quick second where Luc's wolf pushed forward enough for him to see Cassiel's eyes begin to shift lupine, when it happened. The mating bond between them solidified, the attraction intense and immediate. Two souls wrapping around each other and becoming an unbreakable unit. That was the feeling he'd been waiting for, been worrying over. Her wolf had been so hidden that the bond hadn't been strong enough to truly feel. It was now.

Holy fuck, was it.

"What is that?" Cassiel asked, breathless. Her eyes dilating right before his.

"The mating bond between us. Your wolf is finally strong enough to feel it."

"We feel it all right." Cassiel licked her lips, looking him up and down. Making his body want to respond to hers in ways that were far too inappropriate considering there were children nearby. "I think you being behind me will be a good thing."

Ah, fuck. "I'll take you from behind whenever you like, sweet angel. Just say the word."

Cassiel huffed. "Not what I meant, but good to know."

Luc laughed and pulled her in close, kissing the top of her head. "Enough of this sort of talk. Otherwise, we'll never get to where we need to be. Let's run back to the homestead. We can start your wolf education there."

"So soon?"

"Only if you want to. We have time." Lots of it. Years and years to learn everything about one another. Luc was looking forward to every second, too.

Cassiel didn't seem convinced. "Promise? You're not going to, like, overpower me or be all controlling about this stuff?"

"Never."

"And no more lying, right?"

"I never wanted to lie to you. I will never deceive you again. I promise."

"Good, because if you do, I'll cut your balls off."

Luc grimaced. "That's fair."

And it was. She deserved to be loved and respected, which Luc planned to do every day for the rest of his very long and suddenly very interesting life.

"Come on, mate," she said, turning and strutting toward her sled. Rolling her hips in a way that made his mouth water as his eyes locked on her ass. "You can chase me all the way home."

And he would. Forever, if need be.

"Lead the way, mate. I am ready to be your follower."

Epilogue

*I*t took Cassiel six months to learn to shift to her wolf form on her own. Six long months of forced shifts and Alpha orders, of sore muscles and tired bones. Luc never wavered in his support, though. Never questioned whether she'd ever get it. He simply told her how well she was doing after every shift and rubbed her body to ease her aches.

Oh, and how he could make her ache.

"Are you just playing, or are we about to get serious?" her sleepy mate asked as she rocked slowly over his naked body. She loved waking him up like this, with soft touches and kisses, with her pussy gliding over his morning erection. He loved it too, no matter how much he grumbled about her being a tease.

"Just playing. Where are the dogs, by the way?"

"I took them outside a few hours ago. Moxie kept trying to crawl in between us."

Cassiel chuckled, picturing exactly what he described. Her littlest sled dog loved both of them and always wanted to be with them, but that love could cause some awkward moments. Plus, Luc didn't like to share her—not even with an overly affectionate sled dog.

"I should probably go feed them," she said, not that she had any intentions of stopping what she was doing.

Luc groaned, moving his hips to meet hers. Teasing her just as much as she was him. "They're fine out there. They can wait an hour."

"You think you have the stamina for an hour?" She knew he did. He'd proven it many, many times. But she certainly liked to egg him on.

Luc grinned, then grabbed her by the hips, rolling them over into the furs on their bed. The big one they'd had brought out on the ice road once winter had hardened the path and Luc had carved a headboard for. The thing took up half of her cabin, but it didn't matter. Nothing mattered but that she and Luc were together.

Which was why she sighed and grabbed him tighter when he pinned her down and slid inside her wet heat.

"Oh, my angel," he said, growling his words. "You make me so happy."

She nodded, biting his shoulder. Reminding him of the scar embedded there from the night they'd exchanged mating bites. Making sure he remembered he was hers. Her own bite mark stood out proudly on her neck, Luc wanting to make sure every male wolf in the world knew she was taken.

Silly man.

"More," she cried, digging her fingers into his hips. "I need more."

And he gave it.

Ninety minutes and three rounds of amazing sex later, the two of them were finally ready to face the day. Coffee in hand, they were about to head out to feed the dogs when the tablet Deus had gotten them—the one hooked up to some sort of fancy satellite internet he'd bitched and moaned about but that Cassiel though was pretty darn amazing—pinged.

"It's early," Luc said, looking concerned.

Cassiel tapped the screen, smiling as Sariel's face filled it. "Well, hello there, momma."

Sariel's grin grew. "Hi. I know it's early there, but Dina wanted to call Uncle Luc."

Luc moved in beside Cassiel, grabbing her ass in the process. Dirty boy. "How is my brave little shewolf?"

Dina appeared on the screen, obviously climbing into Sariel's lap to see the screen. "I lost a tooth!"

Luc's grin lit up the cabin. "Oh, my girl…such good news. You must be so excited."

"I am. On the television, I saw where, if I put the tooth under my pillow, a fairy will sneak inside my room at night and take it from me."

"Well, yes. That's a very human custom."

Dina growled. "Daddy Bez said no one can penetrate his walls, so I'm keeping my tooth."

Cassiel hid her face, fighting hard not to laugh.

"She's a fierce little soldier," Bez said, appearing behind his mate. The other two girls bounced into the picture as well, all three of them looking so much healthier and happier than they had been when they'd been found. Texas and being in the Dire Wolf pack had been good for them, and finding them had been good for Luc. As had living off the grid and far enough away from most people for him to be able to focus on his own emotions instead of other people's. He still sensed his pack, sensed Cassiel as well, but most of the rest of the world had quieted for him. He liked to tell Cassiel that she was the best thing for him, but she had a feeling living so far from masses of people was right up there, too.

"Did you hear from Phego?" Bez asked, leaning closer to the screen. "Michaela's pregnant."

"We heard," Luc said, clinging to Cassiel. "Our pack is growing."

And they were. Besides Cassiel's own appearance and the three girls, Amy had given birth to a bouncing baby boy with silver eyes and a wolf spirit stronger than any they'd ever seen, according to Luc. Zoe and Charmaine were pregnant as well, both due within just a few weeks of each other. The Dire Pack was definitely growing, and seeing how much joy that brought to Luc made Cassiel's heart happy. She had a family for the first time in her life—a real one.

"So, with all the babies and other issues, we haven't gotten to talk about Australia," Bez said, suddenly looking a little stern. "I know you said we'd go once things calmed down but…"

There was no need to continue that *but*—everyone in the pack would understand it. *But* there were little girls to protect, babies and new moms, too. No one would want to leave their mate behind, and the potential danger could be intense. She and Luc had talked about it many times, laid out options for how they would be the ones to go. The ones to see if there truly was another Dire Wolf pack out there in the world.

The rest of the pack didn't know anything about their plans yet, though.

"There's no need to rush anything," Luc said, squeezing her arm. "Everyone needs time to settle into their new lives, and the children need the structure of their family around them. Dires have lived on this earth for multiple millennia. They'll be there when we're ready."

Which was in about a month, if Luc was still sticking to the last timeline they'd discussed.

"What if they come here first?" Bez asked.

"Then we'll take care of them. Until then, we have lives to live and mates to take care of. I suggest you focus on that."

Luc reached toward the tablet. "Go spoil those angel girls, Beelzebub. I have dogs to feed."

Bez laughed. "Yes, sir."

Luc ended the connection then kissed her neck, taking a moment to breathe her in. "Still okay with heading Down Under for a bit?"

Cassiel tugged him closer. "Absolutely, so long as you're with me."

"I'll never leave your side."

"Then we'll go, and we'll explore. And we'll look for your Dire brothers."

"They might not want us to find them."

"Then we'll use the time to explore a new land. I've always wanted to see a kangaroo in person."

"Then you shall. But for now, we need to feed the dogs."

So they did. And Cassiel couldn't have been happier than she was with her mate at her side doing something so basic as chores around her homestead.

Australia would be coming soon enough. For now, there was Alaska and sled dogs and planes to meet up with. And a mate she couldn't stop touching.

"Race you to the smoking shed," she said, laughing as she took off running. Knowing there was no way she would beat Luc anywhere. He would never let her get too far away either. And that safety net, that security, might have been the best thing she'd ever experienced.

Her mate, her life, her world—perfection wasn't a strong enough word. Australia would happen soon enough, but the where for her didn't matter. For she would follow Luc to the ends of the earth if need be.

She'd also yank him back from the edge of the cliffs of insanity if the world became too much for him.

Protection went both ways after all, and she certainly wasn't one to run away from a fight.

Acknowledgments

This book and this entire series would not have been possible without the kindness and support of my OG reader group members. I call them "My Ladies" and they're some of the nicest, funniest women ever. Thank you to Teri, Terry, Judy, Stephanie, Fran, and Mary for always being there when I need someone to remind me why I spend so much time staring at my computer trying to make words flow. Thank you for the hugs, the kind words, and thee excitement for every book. You all have a very special place in my heart.

Thank you to Lisa Hollett with Silently Correcting Your Grammar for your honesty and critique when I mess up. I hope you enjoyed that extra $24!

That's it. Bye bye, Dire Wolves, Maybe I'll see you again sometimes, or maybe it's time for them to head off into the forest and live out the rest of lives in peace. I'll miss Bez, Levi, Mammon, Thaus, Phego, Deus, and Luc. My demons with their angel mates. My sinners. My Devil's Dires.

About
the Author

A storyteller from the time she could talk, *USA Today* bestsellng author Ellis Leigh grew up among family legends of hauntings, psychics, and love spanning decades. Those stories didn't always have the happiest of endings, so they inspired her to write about real life, real love, and the difficulties therein. From farmers to werewolves, store clerks to witches—if there's love to be found, she'll write about it. Ellis lives in the Chicago area with her husband, daughters, and a German Shepherd that never leaves her side.

www.ellisleigh.com

A *Dire Wolves* MISSION

9 781944 336776